TURF WAR

TURF WAR

RENAY JACKSON

Frog, Ltd.
Berkeley, California

Published by Frog, Ltd.

Frog, Ltd. books are distributed by
North Atlantic Books
P.O. Box 12327
Berkeley, California 94712

Book design by Maxine Ressler
Cover illustrations © 2005 by Ariel Shepard
Cover photo by Peter Graham

Printed in the United States of America

Distributed to the book trade by Publishers Group West

North Atlantic Books' publications are available through most bookstores. For further information, call 800-337-2665 or visit our website at www.northatlanticbooks.com.

Substantial discounts on bulk quantities are available to corporations, professional associations, and other organizations. For details and discount information, contact our special sales department.

Library of Congress Cataloging-in-Publication Data

Jackson, Renay, 1959–
   Turf War / by Renay Jackson.
      p. cm.
   ISBN 1-58394-108-8 (pbk.)
   1. African American criminals — Fiction. 2. Oakland (Calif.) — Fiction.
3. Drug traffic — Fiction. I. Title.
   PS3610.A3547T87 2004
   813'.6 — dc22

                                                        2004021848

      1 2 3 4 5 6 7 8 9 DATA 10 09 08 07 06 05

Dedicated to Johnny Ray Young.

Thanks for all the lessons Bro.
Your little brother learned well.

Rest in peace.

The tongue is but three inches long,
yet can kill a man six feet tall.

—Japanese saying

AUTHOR'S NOTE

This book is based totally on the writer's imagination. Any similarities to actual events are purely coincidental. Although many of the locations are real, they were used only to make the story believable.

SHOUTS

READERS NATIONWIDE WHO
ENJOY MY WORK, THANK YOU

CARLA RIVERS — ONE OF MY MOST
TRUTHFUL CRITICS

NORTH ATLANTIC BOOKS/FROG, LTD. —
FOR BELIEVING IN THE GHETTO FROG (ME)

MISS PATSY — THANX MOMMIE

ANYONE I MISSED — GOD KNOWS,
THANK YOU ALL

TABLE OF CONTENTS

1
STRAIGHT PLAYAS

It was another hot Saturday at the Jamaican Arms apartment complex. Children frolicked all around the swimming area. Little kids jumped around in the shallow end, having water fights, while teenagers showed off their athletic prowess in the deep end. Many of the men sat inside the gated area drinking beer and talking about sports until the sun forced them to seek cooler spots under the palm trees. The women remained on the pool's deck, applying lotion and oils to every exposed part of their body. The water was blue as the sky but looked even more appealing due to the eighty-degree heat.

Located in San Leandro on Doolittle Drive a few blocks from the marina, Jamaican Arms is a huge housing complex with at least fifty units; they have everything from studios to three-bedroom town homes. Each apartment has a patio or terrace, depending on its location and/or size. Beautiful palm trees are situated throughout, along with neatly manicured lawns.

Silky and Junebug stood in the living room staring intently through the picture window at the pool activities. Of particular interest were the honeys rubbing each other's backs with suntan oil. Silky knew it would be only a matter of time before his hands were the ones doing the rubbing. First he wanted to check out all the building had to offer.

Duane "Silky" Johnson was a bonafide ladies' man. Born with a gift for gab, he was given the nickname by his mother Irma when he was ten. She noticed his ability to smooth-talk his way into or out of any situation. She'd often comment to her friends, "That boy is smooth as silk." Naturally everyone started calling him Silky.

In junior high school, Silky began to realize that he could talk girls out of their lunch. Any mistake he made would only improve his game, because Silky Johnson never made the same mistake twice.

By the time he reached high school graduation, Silky would have only the prettiest women at his or another school on his arm. There was not a girl who knew him that did not want to be seen with Silky. His explanation to his mom was that "once they see you with the best there is, Mama, females want to know what you know or what it is you got so special. Now see, that's when I hook 'em."

Standing six-foot-two and weighing a muscular two hundred and ten pounds, he possessed an air of royalty.

When Silky walked into a room, everyone took notice. With a cocoa-butter-brown complexion and piercing jet-black eyes, he zoomed in on his prey without blinking. His hair was full, thick, and styled in a "Lord Jesus" perm. Black, shoulder length, and with a patch of gold dyed along the back edges, that head of hair never seemed to have a strand out of place.

Around his neck hung a solid gold rope chain with a Holy Cross pendant. Today Silky wore a gold rayon shirt with red, burgundy, and turquoise designs, buttoned halfway up to expose his hairy chest. Gold slacks, belt, socks, and Stacy Adams gave him the fly look he desired daily. Whatever color pants Silky wore, his entire outfit would match. His left hand displayed one humongous gold cluster ring on the middle finger; a Rolex watch graced his wrist. The right had a custom-made 14-carat gold ring spelling out "SILKY," which was fitted on two fingers. A gold-link nugget bracelet dangled from that wrist.

Anthony "Junebug" Grimes had been Silky's road dog since they were twelve years old. If Junebug had half the game as his partner, he would have had twice as many women. He was the perfect sidekick because he never got jealous of his homey. He was just as flashy a dresser with the same impeccable grooming habits. Most women considered him pretty while classifying Silky as handsome. Junebug just didn't have Silky's game.

He stood six-one, one ninety-five, with a "Lord" hairdo, sideburns down to his jawbone, and a thick black mustache and goatee. All that thick black hair only accented his high yellow complexion. He was decked out in a burgundy rayon shirt with blue and gold designs, burgundy slacks, belt, socks, and shoes. The two men stood peering out the window while sipping drinks. Junebug had a brandy and coke while Silky drank orange juice on the rocks.

Junebug headed for the kitchen to refill his shot while Silky continued to gaze out through the window. He hated it when his homey hit the booze early because it limited his effectiveness. Silky never drank alcohol — to him that was taboo. He knew booze separated his game from Junebug's because once you were under the influence, your brain wasn't as sharp as it needed to be.

"Man, you picked a cool location for the crib," Junebug said.

"I know, I came up big-time, boy," Silky boasted.

"Which one of those gray girls you want?"

"Don't know yet, 'Bug."

"Know that's right!" They slapped five.

"I'll tell you what, dude."

"What's that, Silk?"

"When I do choose, the girl gonna feel blessed."

"Gray Girl" is an expression black dudes use to describe white women. Why? Who knows. Yet and still, that's what they are called.

Silky had moved from Oaktown to nearby San Leandro three weeks earlier. The apartment manager, a fifty-year-old mother of three with white hair and a pudgy build, was struck by his piercing eyes and good looks. In less than ten minutes Silky had her doing everything possible to provide him a place. She filled out his application, waived his credit check fee, and wrote up a rental agreement on the spot.

She mistakenly thought he desired her physically, because she definitely wanted a piece of him. Her husband was livid when he found out she'd rented to a spade. After slapping her around, he double-checked every form hoping to find some error that he could use to deny Silky's move. Resigned to the fact that his friends would blame him, he picked up the daily paper and scanned the want ads for apartment managers. They would be long gone by the time Silky moved in.

Oaktown is only a stone's throw from San Leandro, but the comparisons end there. Oaktown is predominantly black and Mexican, with numerous other nationalities thrown in for good measure. Poverty is on every corner along with welfare, unemployment, and crime.

San Leandro is white and wealthy. Crime rates are low, section 8 is called subsidized housing, and most people hold jobs. Three weeks earlier when Silky moved in, he couldn't help noticing all the angry looks from his new white neighbors. Blacks were beginning to migrate there to escape the ghetto, so Silky figured that he may as well be the first one on his block.

"Man, would you look at that!" Junebug drooled.

"That's the one," Silky stated matter-of-factly.

The object of their attention was a gray girl who'd just entered the pool area. She was a statuesque blond with hair flowing halfway down her back. Six feet tall with milk-white skin, she had almond-shaped auburn eyes, full pouty lips, and a thin pointy nose. The other women treated her like the queen bee, vying for her attention.

A super-sized towel covered her body, and when she pulled it off Junebug let out a whistle.

"Damn, Silky, how did you get a crib right in front of the pool? Talk about location!"

The girl had a body you would kill for, 36-24-36. Her breasts were large and spilling out of the skimpy bikini bra she wore. The nipples were at least half an inch long. Silky wondered if they were red, pink, brown, or black. She had a washboard stomach, nice round butt, and a mouth-watering gap between her legs, which were long and thick. A gold-link anklet and pink painted toenails gave her the classy look Silky loved in women. The girl had it goin' on; there was no doubting that.

She neatly spread her towel on the deck then reached into an oversized bag and pulled out a bottle of suntan oil, which she applied liberally to her skin. Silky watched every move like a hawk visualizing what he intended to do to his prey. After putting sunglasses over her eyes, she stretched out on her back and got her tan.

"How you gonna mack that, player?" Junebug asked his friend.

"I'll let the game come to me."

"You might have to take the game to that fox, homes."

"Junebug, you just sit back and take notes 'cause class is in session."

"What about her man? You know she got one!"

"Dude, as long as you've known me, have you ever known me to worry about some broad's man?"

"Not the Silky I know."

They spent the next few minutes talking head to each other. The braggadocio between these two was always animated, with each man trying to top the other's version of past sexual conquests. All they really accomplished was getting themselves aroused while watching all that white meat prance around outside.

Silky told Junebug, "Let's go check my mailbox."

They put on their shades and walked out the door. Looking as cool as cool could be, Silky and Junebug strutted past the pool, getting more than casual looks from its occupants. Nonchalantly, they ignored the scene. As they strolled past the men, whatever conversation was going on ceased as all eyes rested on the two brothers. Once they were out of earshot, the conversation was them.

Silky's mailbox was empty, so they headed across the street to the store. Marina Faire Shopping Center is one of those quaint little strip malls that white neighborhoods always have but black communities can never get. Its tenants included All-American Market, a full-fledged supermarket specializing in off-brand products.

There was a tanning salon, pizza parlor, liquor store, donut shop, travel agency, shoe repair shop, video rental store, nightclub, delicatessen, and assorted small businesses that changed owners and names constantly. They walked into the liquor store, purchased a package of Zigzags, then headed back across Doolittle towards the crib.

Suddenly Silky blurted out, "Let's take a ride."

"That'll work," replied his partner.

They hopped into Silky's ride, a '93 Jeep Cherokee Laredo. He called it "The Black Mongoose," not caring or knowing that a mongoose is a snake- and rat-eating animal from India. To Silky, "The Black Mongoose" sounded fly. As his new white neighbors watched, they eased into the flow of traffic. Taking into consideration how young Silky looked and the fact that he had his own apartment plus a brand new hoopty, the residents of Jamaican Arms immediately labeled him a drug dealer/bad element.

"Where we rolling to, dog?" Junebug asked while lighting up a joint.

"I think we'll pay a visit to the twins," he replied.

"Yeah, let's see what those hoes talkin 'bout."

"'Bug, they ain't no hoes, fool, those are two classy ladies."

"You say what you want, boss, I say they hoes."

The Mongoose hit 880 and headed towards Oaktown with Boyz II Men blaring out of the sound system.

"'Bug, why is it all the women we know are hoes to you?"

"Silk Master, a hoe is a hoe, is a motherfuckin hoe, niggah."

"It ain't got ta be like that, Junebug." Silky liked this type of banter between them.

"See Silky, you be tryin ta make them hoes fall in love with you. Now, on the other hand, I'm tryin ta get paid. When and if you learn that shit, yo game gone be strong as mine." Junebug believed his logic.

"Junebug, you my boy, you know that, right?" Silky asked.

"You motherfuckin right," Junebug stated emphatically.

"Then for as long as you've known me, how can you fix your lips to say you got more game than me? Fool, I could take every woman you got if I wanted to, and you better believe the only reason I don't is because you my boy."

Junebug laughed loudly while striking his leg with his hand. Passing the joint to Silky, he said, "Man, this shit so good, you high off the fumes already."

They both cracked up. The "my game top yo game" banter continued until they reached the twins' apartment complex. Getting out of the Mongoose, they strutted up the walkway to the security gate telephone. Silky picked up the receiver then dialed. After the second ring, someone answered.

"Hello." The voice was sexy.

"Hey boo, it's me, Silky."

The buzzer sounded on the gate and Junebug opened it as Silky placed the phone back on the holder. The twins resided on Vernon Avenue, three blocks from Lake Merritt. Apartments lined the entire block, which was not unusual for this high-rent district. Their building was painted lime with a dark green trim. Named "Bermuda" and consisting of ten identical two-bedroom flats along with a courtyard swimming pool, the place was neat in appearance and quiet.

Silky was first to the door, which was slightly ajar, so he entered with his homey right behind.

"Hey baby," said Neisha, greeting Silky with a kiss.

"Hello, love." He held her close.

Neisha Davis was dressed in a form-fitting spandex one-piece. Royal blue, it appeared to have been painted on.

"Hey Junebug, how you doin?"

"I'm cool, Nee — where's Kee?" Junebug asked.

"Keisha's in the shower, she'll be out in a minute. Would you guys like me to get you anything?"

"Naw baby, we're cool. I just stopped by to see if we were still on for tonight?" Silky's question was more of a statement.

"Yes babes, we wouldn't miss it for the world."

"OK, then be ready at eight!" he said.

Silky and Junebug turned to leave when Keisha strutted in.

"Hello Junebug, Silky — did I miss something?" She gave Junebug a peck on the cheek.

Keisha wore a bone-colored outfit that hugged every inch of her frame. Identical twins, the only thing that distinguished one from the other was their hair styles. Keisha's mane flowed while Neisha preferred finger waves.

They both were beautiful. High yellow with hazel eyes, full lips, and sculpted bodies, the twins had it going on. Mirror images of each other, they dressed, thought, and acted as one.

"No, you didn't," answered Silky. "We were just making sure it's still on for tonight."

"Of course it's on, that is unless you two fake," responded Keisha.

"Just be ready!" Silky said. "Come on, 'Bug, let's go."

"You're not staying?" Keisha questioned.

"No, we have things to do, but we'll be back, baby," Junebug stated.

The twins watched from the door as Silky and Junebug strolled through the courtyard. By the time they got to the Mongoose, the girls were already debating what outfits they would wear. Silky put the key into the ignition, started the engine, and cruised away.

2
IT AIN'T OVER

Shakey Jones sat on a top bunk in the bullpen, still furious because of his arrest. He knew he hadn't killed anybody, so he felt like it was only a matter of time before his release.

Shakey had been arrested and charged with the murder of Nadine McCoy, his former girlfriend. He didn't love her; she was just a pawn in his chess game, being used as bait to get back the affection of his ex-wife Cassandra. He didn't know who killed Nadine, but he figured it must have been Big Ed or one of his flunkeys.

Calvin "Shakey" Jones was a powerful man. Standing six-two on a rock-solid two hundred-and-forty-pound frame, he looked bigger due to all the weightlifting done over the years. Thick cornrow braids adorned his scalp, accenting high cheekbones, big lips, and a goatee. A midnight-black complexion and evil stare immediately left the impression of a stereotypical jailbird.

The past week's activities saw Shakey being released from prison and moving in with Nadine, only to leave her for another woman. He also began selling crack on a turf controlled by a gang known as the Eastside Empire. The eventual turf war that had erupted in Shakey's wake had already resulted in numerous deaths. Nadine and Shakey's hit man Robert "Slack" Henderson were two of the casualties.

The news of Slack's death hit Shakey hard and left no doubt in his mind that Ed Tatum was behind it. Since "Big Ed" was the leader of the Eastside Empire, he had to die. Slack had been Shakey's lifelong partner, so there was no doubt that his murder would be avenged.

Sheila Rae Duncan, Shakey's new woman, proved her mettle by providing him with an indisputable alibi, so she was down for the count. Thanks to her, Five-O (a term for the police) would have to release him within seventy-two hours. The only way Shakey could be detained was if new evidence linking him to Nadine's death were found. Since he didn't commit the murder, the police would come up empty and have no choice but to set him free.

Shakey watched with little interest as all the fellow inmates played dominoes, cards, checkers and chess. His mind was on Big Ed and revenge. When the steel doors opened to let new prisoners enter, Shakey's attention was on the television newscast sensationalizing the past week's murders.

Eventually glancing towards the door at the new arrivals, Shakey noticed Big Ed, who spotted Shakey at the same time. Big Ed stood six-five and carried three hundred pounds on a granite frame. A former all-city football player and wrestler, he was a very violent individual.

Big Ed wanted Shakey just as bad as Shakey wanted him because in Big Ed's opinion, if that fool hadn't attempted to move in on his turf, none of this drama would have occurred. In one week of the drug war he lost three top lieutenants along with three personal henchmen. Naturally, he held Shakey responsible.

Hopping off his bunk, Shakey strode over to his rival and stared him down. Everyone scattered because the tension was so thick you could cut it with a knife. Without a word spoken between the two, it was on. . . .

Shakey got off first, landing a crushing blow to the jaw. Big Ed retaliated with a bone-crunching right hand to the forehead. Shakey threw another right that landed just below the eye, then received a return shot that knocked him back three steps. Regrouping, he faked a right and connected with a left hook that was picture-perfect.

The next minute was spent with each man throwing his best punches and the other accepting, only to return one of his own. Since Shakey was from the west side of town and Big Ed from the east, battle lines were drawn among the inmates, who formed a circle around the combatants. The action in the center ring reminded everyone of the Hearns-Hagler second round, where neither man gave an inch.

Big Ed bumrushed Shakey, grabbing him in a bear hug.

Shakey locked his arms over Ed's, curling them around the armpits and attempting to throw him down, but it didn't work. Big Ed lifted Shakey off his feet, body-slamming his rival onto the cement floor. The two men began rolling over, with each one seeking to gain control. Everyone knew that whoever came out on top would beat the mess out of the other man.

A hand reached in from the crowd, pulling Shakey's leg, which effectively gave Big Ed the advantage. This singular action resulted in fights breaking out all over the joint. Most of the older Negroes and Mexicans sat on their bunks watching with amusement while blacks were hurting blacks. Big Ed wound up on top, pinning down Shakey's arms with his knees.

Just as he was about to peel Shakey's cap, twenty officers dressed in riot gear charged into the room swinging billyclubs at anything moving. Everyone scattered as they controlled the situation with force. It took four officers to hold down Shakey and six for Big Ed.

"It ain't over, muthafucka!" shouted Ed.

"You gone die, bitch!" screamed Shakey.

"You lucky they came in, boy, 'cause ah was fitna put a hurtin on yo ass!"

"Right, you fool, wit help! Yo boys knowed ah was 'bout ta stomp a mudhole in yo ass so dey pulled mah leg."

"Aw fuck you, niggah, you gone die!" hollered Big Ed as he was hauled away.

Big Ed and Shakey were both escorted to solitary cells, along with six additional inmates who'd participated in the fracas. The remaining prisoners would have a jailhouse story to tell for the rest of their lives. They were already tying up the collect-call phone lines to give their women blow-by-blow details, along with lying about what role they played.

Shakey sat in his cell holding his head, which was still ringing from the blows he'd absorbed. He was like a pit bull licking his wounds and just waiting for the next dog-fight. Big Ed sat in his cell feeling the same type of pain. He'd never been hit that much during a rumble.

"Calvin Jones, you're free to go," the jailer said as he opened the cell door a few hours later. "Follow me."

Shakey trailed the officer down the narrow hallway to the property window. There, he signed out for his belongings and was handed a ziplock bag, which he immediately opened. Placing his wallet, money, and keys into his pockets, he put his rings, rope, watch, and bracelet on his body, then tossed the baggie into a trash can.

The sound of the final steel door slamming behind him brought a smile to his face. Being released from jail always had that effect on Shakey Jones. Now he was free to eat when he wanted, go where he chose, bathe without some pervert looking at his booty, and shit in peace.

Sheila sat patiently on a bench in the lobby. She appeared to be out of her element due to the fact that most of the people waiting there were dressed shabbily. She wore a form-fitting blue acrylic dress, which prominently displayed wide hips and a very large butt.

As she rose to greet Shakey, the talking amongst the others ceased. Standing six feet two inches tall on a slender frame, Sheila Rae Duncan commanded attention. She had a peanut-butter complexion with catlike eyes and a small nose. Her nails and toes were polished candy-apple red, and she displayed attitude.

As she walked over to her man, her behind switched with every step. The movement of her butt was not calculated, just natural. Sheila Rae represented sex, and everyone in the lobby knew it. As the men gawked at her physique, their women drooled at Shakey's chiseled frame.

"Ooh baby, it's so good to see you," Sheila said as she kissed her man.

"It's good to see you too," Shakey responded.

"What happened in there?" she asked.

"What you mean, babes?"

"Look at you, you been fightin!"

"Aw it ain't shit, dat fool know he on mah list now."

"What fool?" Sheila shouted.

"Big Ed."

"Shakey, what went on in there?"

"I'll tell you later — let's get the hell outta here."

As they headed out the plate-glass door Sheila surveyed the bruises and lumps on Shakey's face. Grimacing, she cupped her arm inside his bent elbow and walked to the car. Shakey followed her lead but his mind was still on Big Ed. He got in the passenger side, then spoke.

"What happened wit Slack?" he asked.

"I don't know, baby; I dropped him off at the garage, then the next morning Yolanda found him dead."

"Damn!" he shouted. "When's the funeral?"

"The date hasn't been set but the state will pay for it."

"They will?" He was surprised.

"Yes, they have some sort of fund that pays the costs of burial for victims of violent homicides."

"Oh, ah didn't know dat." Shakey scratched his head. "Did the police search the garage?"

"Yes, but Yolanda gave me your dope and money before they did."

"Cool," he stated.

The remainder of the drive home was spent with Shakey reclining his car seat and closing his eyes. He was tired and his woman knew it so she drove as if she were alone. She pulled into her assigned stall at the "court" and parked.

Chestnut Court is one of many housing projects in Oaktown. Painted purple with lavender trim, it is the fifth-largest housing complex on the west side. The court, as it's called, is built like a fortress. Three stories high, it spans an entire city block, housing at least fifty units.

A driveway on Linden Street allows those with cars to park in the center lot, which covers half the landscape. The other half is occupied by a city-run childcare facility, along with children's sandlot. As Shakey and Sheila got out of the car, they noticed a guy knocking on Sheila's door.

"Is that the 'friend' you tole me 'bout?" Shakey spewed through clenched teeth.

"Yes, honey, that's Marcus, but I don't know what he wants. I haven't talked to him since I met you."

"Well, you gone hafta tell 'im he cain't come roun heah no moe."

"O.K.," Sheila said as they headed up to her third-floor unit.

Marcus Robinson stood at Sheila's door looking passive and hurt. He'd only known her for a year but had fallen madly in love, even though he knew she didn't feel the same affection toward him. Seeing her with another man broke his heart. Common sense told him to leave, but his ego made him stay — the dude just might be her brother or something.

"Marcus, what are you doing?" Sheila asked angrily.

"I came to see you," he stated. "Aren't you going to introduce me?"

"Look Marcus, I've told you repeatedly to call me before coming to my place unannounced."

"I did call but your answering machine came on."

"Then you should have left a message."

"Look dude, you gone hafta leave," Shakey demanded.

"Let the lady tell me that," Marcus responded.

Shakey fired off a punch, which connected squarely on Marcus' jaw. The force of the blow knocked him down. He attempted to get up but was greeted by another right hand to the mouth. Blood poured from his lip as Shakey kicked him savagely in the ribs.

"Now is you gone leave or get stomped?" Shakey growled.

Sheila stood covering her mouth with her hands, frightened by the scene. She had never witnessed this side of her man. His actions were so swift and brutal that she didn't know what to do.

"I'm lea-leave-leaving!" Marcus cried out.

Struggling to his feet, Marcus staggered to the stairwell bloody and punch-drunk. Shakey still wasn't done. He took his foot and kicked Marcus in the small of the back, causing him to tumble down the steps to the next landing. Shakey made a move to go after him, but Sheila grabbed his arm.

"Baby wait, he's leaving," she pleaded.

"Ah know, but ah'mo make sho he don't come back."

Marcus scrambled to his feet and hurried groggily down the stairs. When he got to the bottom he turned around, only to be greeted by a thundering right hand to the forehead. By now, most of the building tenants were watching the drama unfold.

In the ghetto, this sort of madness happens daily, so the scene horrified no one. They just silently hoped Marcus would turn and run. Shakey chose not to beat him down, instead opting to beat him off the complex. Every time Marcus got up and staggered a few steps, Shakey would knock him back on his ass. His attempts to block punches proved futile.

Satisfied with his work, Shakey headed back up the steps to his woman. People went back inside their units to resume what they were doing before being interrupted. Marcus got in his car and sat there until his head stopped ringing. Pulling off, he vowed never to return.

"Shakey, you didn't have to beat him like that!" Sheila said with tears streaming down her cheeks.

"Ah tole you ta tell his ass what's up," he whispered.

"But he was leaving!" she screamed.

"Dat ass-whuppin was ta make sho he don't come back."

Sheila opened the door and went in as Shakey followed. The moment she turned around, he pulled her body to his and gave her a hungry kiss. The longer they kissed, the more her anger melted, turning into passion and desire. Her body raged like a fire out of control.

"Ah needs ta take a baff," Shakey said as he headed for the bathroom.

"Don't be long," Sheila said while undressing.

Shakey showered, rubbed himself down with baby oil, then strutted into the bedroom. Sheila peeped out his glistening muscles and the weapon between his legs, then sensuously pulled back the cover for him. He joined her in bed and proceeded to plow into her body with urgency. She loved every minute of it.

He was the first man to take her over the edge since her husband died. Sheila's sexual appetite was voracious, but Shakey proved to be a full-course meal. Exhausted, they lay in each other's arms, drifting off into a peaceful sleep.

WHO'S THE MAN?

"Silky did WHAT?" shouted Skye.

"Yeah boss, fool told all yo boys he runnin da show now," stated Lou.

"Oh, he runnin thangs, huh? I'mo kick Silky's ass!"

Skye Barnes considered himself the new kingpin after the arrest of his boss Big Ed Tatum. Systematically, he'd successfully taken over the east-side drug empire. Most of the empire's associates played along, not wanting a rift with Skye.

All of the top-level dealers in the organization were murdered recently during the violent drug war, and Skye was the main one left. Since his dope house was the number-one moneymaker and he knew the program inside out, he took over by attrition.

Silky was of a different mindset. He believed that the best man should be in control based on merit, not seniority. Of course, he considered himself the best man. Skye lacked entrepreneurial skills and had no clue about expansion. To Silky, that justified his logic.

Standing five feet eight inches short, Skye was built like a fireplug. He ran his turf violently and had a bad attitude along with a nastier temper. His physique resembled Mike Tyson's.

He was a deadly individual and everyone knew it. If a client "forgot" to pay a debt, an associate's trap was short, or someone peddled dope on the turf without buying it from him, Skye would personally beat 'em down. He took pleasure in hurting people.

"Lou."

"Yeah, Skye?"

"Next time you lay eyes on that fool, call me immediately."

"Awight," Lou agreed.

Skye had known Lou all his life and considered him his only true friend. If the dictionary were to list a definition of road dogs, their mugs would be prominently displayed. Regarding each other as cousins, Skye and Lou were inseparable. The similarities ended there: Lou was passive, laid back, and thought things through, while Skye was aggressive, emotional, and acted on impulse.

Louis Arterberry pumped fear into no one. Although the boy's facial features looked scary, his demeanor was passive. He stood five-ten and weighed a soft one-sixty due to lack of exercise and weightlifting.

A cocoa complexion was accented by high cheekbones, huge nostrils, dark deep-set eyes, mustache, and beard.

His lips were large, and when he talked one couldn't help but notice the two missing front teeth. Lou's street tag was "Toothless," and everybody called him that except Skye. He was a known coward, but when Skye was around, Lou would clown in a minute. He knew his partner would take up for him — so did everyone else, for that matter.

Since Skye was now running the show, he'd placed Lou in charge of his turf, which ran from Fruitvale to 82nd Avenue. It was the most lucrative operation, and Skye intended to keep it that way. Basically he gave Lou a title but continued to oversee the business.

"Muggsy, if you see that fool, call me — you too, Damon!" Skye barked. "We gonna settle this shit once and for all."

"Awight," Muggsy said.

Isaiah "Muggsy" Caldwell was a bonafide slickster. Any opportunity that arose to use or run game on someone, Muggsy took advantage. He stood six feet even on a healthy two-hundred-pound frame. Cocoa brown, Muggsy wore a low-cut afro with sideburns down to his jawbone, along with a neatly trimmed mustache and goatee.

Decked out in black Levis pressed to a crisp with a matching silk shirt and ankle-high boots, Muggsy always looked clean. He wore several ropes of various sizes and designs around his neck, along with a gold watch, link bracelet, and two sparkling rings on each hand.

The diamond-studded earring displayed on his lobe glistened with any movement of his head, and when he opened his mouth, all you saw were gold caps on his front teeth. Muggsy's eyes were shifty, always looking around; his senses stayed on alert like radar. Those who made the mistake of letting their guard down, male or female, would be played like a deck of cards. Skye didn't trust Muggsy because he knew the fool was slick; however, he felt like the dude had sense enough not to cross him.

Muggsy picked up his leather golf cap, pulling it low on his forehead, and put on his waist-length leather jacket. "Let's raise, Day," he said to his homey.

"I'm down with that," Damon said and rose to leave.

Damon Scott had been dealing dope since the age of thirteen and been a friend of Muggsy's just as long. His rise in the empire was due mainly to his ability to stay one step ahead of the police. If he were an honest working man, his professional skill would have been as an analyst, because he possessed an uncanny ability to forecast trends in the drug trade.

He was the first in the organization to realize the impact that crack cocaine would have on the community. He was also the first to know that methamphetamine (speed) was going to knock crack out the box because it was cheaper to buy and your high lasted longer. Not only that, by the time most people heard of the "Friends Helping Friends" pyramid scheme, Damon had cashed out twice and was out of the game with a cool thirty-two thousand.

Damon stood five-nine on a trim one-hundred-and-eighty-pound frame. His dress habits reminded you of the rap group RUN DMC because he preferred blue Levis, Adidas tennis shoes, button-down rayon shirt, thigh-length leather coat, and matching brim.

Muggsy and Damon had worked as a team their entire criminal career, but now with the sudden changes in the organization, each man would have his own turf to run. Muggsy was placed in charge of the Sobrante Park/Dagg/ Brookfield neighborhoods, which were collectively tagged the "poe folks' turf" due in large part to high crime, unemployment, and poverty. This area took second only to the west side as the poorest in the city.

Damon was assigned the hills, which was the wealthiest neighborhood. His turf ran from 82nd & East 14th to the San Leandro border, including the hills. He and Muggsy had been second in command of this turf for years so all he had to do was continue business as usual. Muggsy, on the other hand, would have to implement a brand-new system because he was now running the lousiest operation. Even with their promotions they remained a tag team, at least for the time being.

"What yaw doin today?" Skye asked.

"Goin to the concert tonight, what else?" Muggsy answered.

"Have fun."

"You ain't goin?" Damon inquired.

"Naw dude, that shit ain't impotant."

"Awight Skye," they said in unison.

Muggsy and Damon walked out "Da Spot," which was the moniker of Skye's drug house. They didn't particularly care for Skye and thought less of his business acumen, but since they wanted no battle with him, he was the man. Da Spot was located on the east side at 65th & Outlook.

"You ain't goin to the concert tonight?" Lou asked Skye.

"Hell naw, I'mo do what I do best, make money."

"Check it, I got two tickets for the show, but if you need me here, I'll tell my girl to take one of her chickenhead friends."

"No, you go ahead," Sky declined.

"Awight boss, I'm fitna go buy me something ta wear."

"Awight!" Skye said as they shook hands.

Lou walked out to his bucket, which was a black '86 Caprice four-door in desperate need of paint. He started the engine and sped off, headed for the mall in San Leandro, where he would spend the next three hours shopping for a "fit" to wear that night.

Skye leaned back in a recliner and lit up a joint of weed. He would spend the rest of the evening getting high and selling dope. Business was slow that evening so Skye had plenty of time to think about Silky. This fact burnt him up because he hated to think about another man.

Just the fact he had that fool on his mind instead of a woman increased his anger. As expected, the effects of the weed gave him the munchies, so he went to the refrigerator and retrieved some leftover catfish and fries he'd bought earlier.

After heating his meal in the microwave, Skye wolfed it down greedily. Then he grabbed the remote and flicked on his television set before sprawling out on the dingy sofa. The telephone rang, ruining what had been a peaceful sleep.

"Hello."

"Skye, it's me, Lou!" came the shout at the other end of the line.

"Whatup dog?"

"Man, that fool in here."

"Who? Silky?" Skye barked.

"Yeah man, I see his ass now!"

"Come get me, Lou."

"Awight, ahm on mah way."

Lou shut off his cell phone, explained to his girl what the deal was and that she should ride home with her friends, then bounced. Skye rose up off the sofa, hurried to the bedroom, grabbed his weapons, and went outside. When Lou drove up Skye was waiting.

Ч
PARTY TIME

Silky maneuvered the Mongoose to an empty stall in the crowded parking lot, then joined Junebug and the twins at the rear of the vehicle. Concertgoers littered the landscape drinking liquor, smoking dope, and blasting their sound systems to the hilt.

MC Smoove would be performing tonight, and when Smoove came home, the atmosphere was always festive. It didn't matter that the show would be at Eastmont Mall instead of the Coliseum — what counted most was there would be a show.

Rap gigs in Oaktown were few and far between these days, due in large part to a handful of knuckleheads who just didn't know how to behave. The Coliseum Arena, which was the largest venue in the city, had not hosted a rap show for at least four years since they always resulted in violence.

People were thrown off balconies, in addition to fistfights erupting in the parking lot, auditorium, and onstage. Chaos reigned, with Five-O unable to control the situation. Two hundred officers against twenty thousand partygoers were slim odds.

However, things always seemed more peaceful at the mall. The shindig was held in the old Mervyn's storefront, which was huge. It reminded you of a large warehouse and provided Eastmont with a fat user fee from the promoters. The interior was spacious, to say the least.

Silky put his arm around Neisha's waist, while Junebug and Keisha walked arm in arm.

"Thanks, baby," Neisha told Silky.

"For what?" he responded.

"For bringing us here, silly," she laughed, and so did her twin.

"Gurlll, only da bess fa yaw," slurred Junebug.

Keisha was developing a strong dislike for Silky's friend because he stayed drunk. She'd already pulled her twin's coattail to the fact that liquor was on his breath earlier that day. They both knew Junebug was a disaster waiting to happen.

The sisters wore black leather skirts so short they nearly revealed the imprint lines the bottom of their behinds made. High-heeled shoes caused their already muscular legs to look even more chiseled. The fact that they were glistening with baby oil instantly made every man in the lot gaze with lust. Their waist-length leather jackets were zipped only halfway up, exposing beautiful cleavage.

Keisha and Neisha were not into excess makeup, fake fingernails, colored contacts, or jewelry. With these two, what you saw is what it was, and what it was — was phine!!! Silky wore a black leather outfit complemented by matching boots, socks, and shirt. His Dobbs brim sat lightly on his head cocked to the side. Saturated in gold, he looked like a pimp. Junebug was decked out in beige, sporting a godfather brim, blazer jacket and slacks, flared-collar shirt, socks and boots. Just like Silky, he was draped.

"Spread 'em," the guard demanded.

The foursome obeyed as other guards scanned their bodies with hand-held metal detectors. Passing inspection, Silky handed over the tickets to the cashier and they all went inside. Booming rap tunes greeted them, along with people dancing everywhere. Giant eight-foot-high speakers were scattered along the walls and in the corners. The music was so loud that in order to be heard you had to yell.

Security patrolled the floor in teams of two. They communicated by radio transmitters and stuck out like a sore thumb in their bright-yellow windbreakers.

A makeshift concession stand was set up at the back of the hall, where a long line of customers waited to buy overpriced eats. The menu consisted of popcorn, hot dog and link sandwiches, potato chips, soft drinks, and candy. Watered-down beer was sprayed into cups from a keg, which didn't seem to matter to the customers, many of whom were drunk before they got there.

The stage sat front and center, four feet high. On it was a DJ spinning all the latest hits, along with a solitary microphone perched at the top of its stand. Since the show would begin shortly, Silky led his folks towards the front of the stage. The night's master of ceremony walked out and picked up the mic.

He sported a royal-blue leather suit, white turtleneck, blue pimp socks, and matching alligator boots. A phat dookie rope hung from his neck, and his white safari hat featured a blue band. His coconut-colored face was oval-shaped with a large nose, pearl-white teeth, and full lips.

"Good evening, ladies and gentlemen," he began, "on behalf of Plug-it Enterprises, I'd like to thank you all for coming out tonight. My name is Johnny Skate, and I'll be your emcee for the affair. We have a great show lined up so get ready to party. Now, I'll ask, yaw ready ta rock?" he crooned.

"Yeah!" the crowd responded enthusiastically.

During his entire spiel, the DJ played rap instrumental beats, which served to keep everyone grooving. Heads bobbed and all eyes were riveted on the stage. By the time the opening artist appeared, the house was at a fever pitch.

Each act was better than the one before, and when MC Smoove hit the platform, the crowd was more than ready. All of the previous performers had dancers, homeboys pumping up the crowd, or backup singers. With Smoove, it would be just a DJ and microphone. He didn't want nor need gimmicks because his raps were that strong.

Smoove strutted out to a rousing ovation and instantly began working the crowd. He stood five-ten and weighed a solid one-seventy-five. A neatly trimmed mustache and goatee accented his peanut-butter skin tone. His hair was finger-waved down to his shoulders, and he had gold loop rings in each ear.

He wore loose-fitting black jeans, basketball sneakers, Raiders jacket, and so much jewelry that you knew he had money. The party rocked, and everyone seemed to be thoroughly enjoying themselves. Of course, security tossed out the few knuckleheads before they created a scene. The ones who were outright obnoxious were led away by Five-O to spend the night behind bars.

Silky spent the whole night cuddled up with Neisha, making her feel like she was the most important woman in the place. They laughed, danced the bump-n-grind, kissed, and put on their own little performance for all the folks stealing glances. Neisha was on a cloud.

Keisha, on the other hand, was miserable because Junebug spent all his time talking with dudes he knew or heading for the concession stand to get another drink. The concert couldn't end quickly enough for her. Disappointed would be too nice a word to describe her mood. She was angry.

"Hey girl, we're going to a club after we leave here, OK?" Neisha said to her twin.

"NO!" Keisha stated boldly.

"Sister, why not?"

"Girl, I wouldn't go to a dogfight with that fool."

"Come on, Keisha, let's have some fun, Silky and me...."

"You and Silky can do as you please, just take me home first," Keisha demanded.

"Where's Junebug?" Neisha asked.

"The hell if I know," her sister answered.

"Wait right here," Neisha said.

Neisha walked over to Silky and began telling him about the rift that had developed between her sister and his homeboy. Silky listened intently before heading towards the concession stand in search of Junebug. He was too upset to notice the pair of eyes following his every move.

"'Bug? Whatup with you and Kee, homes?"

"Silky, fuck dat bish, man."

"Why you say that?" Silky was calm.

"That bish thank she all lat, but ah'll tell ya now, da bish ain't shit," Junebug slurred.

"Damn 'Bug, yo ass sho know how to fuck up a wet dream."

"Oh, you comin at me wit dat love shit again, huh?"

Silky walked away shaking his head in disgust at his drunken friend. When he was straight, Junebug could charm the panties off a honey in a minute. It was the times like now when he swallowed too much booze that he would ruin the best-laid plans. Since he and Silky were road dogs and always together, it was inevitable that his and Keisha's dislike for each other would put a damper on Silky and Neisha's budding relationship.

The concert ended with the foursome heading out the door to the Black Mongoose. Keisha walked in front, arms folded and in a hurry, while Silky and Neisha followed, fingers interlocked. Junebug trailed behind, talking loudly with people he knew. The ride to the twins' pad was spent with each individual silently hoping that Silky could get there faster.

He and Neisha held hands over the armrest in front while Junebug and Keisha sat in the back as far away from each other as possible. The more they thought about the horrible date, the more their hatred of each other grew. Junebug caught Silky's evil glances at him in the rearview mirror but continued to look out the window at the darkened scenery. He pulled out a joint and fired it up.

"Could you at least wait until we get home?" Keisha barked.

"Yes, I could, but I'm not," Junebug growled.

"'Bug, put it out, man" Silky intervened.

Junebug put out the weed and resumed his mumbling to himself in his corner spot. Silky pulled up to the Bermuda complex, got out, then opened the door for Neisha. Before he could do the same for Keisha, she was already entering the security gate.

"Silky, thanks for taking us out," Keisha said as she hurried into the crib.

"No problem, Kee, sorry it didn't work out," he said.

Junebug got out of the back seat and walked around the SUV to the front. Before he got in again he shouted, "Oh, I'ont even get a damn goodbye?" He pulled hard on the weed.

Neisha sighed out loud as she and Silky walked through the courtyard.

"Thanks baby for a nice time," she whispered as she kissed him lovingly. "It's too bad you have to leave."

"Too bad for you or me?" he smiled.

"For the both of us." She kissed him again.

"I'll call you in the morning, OK?"

"Yes honey," she said, then disappeared inside.

Silky headed for his ride and the inevitable argument with his sidekick. Jumping in, he turned the volume down and started in on 'Bug before pulling away.

"Man, you blew that shit tonight, homes, big-time."

"I ain't blew shit, Silky."

"Oh no? What do you call it then?"

"Like I said, the bish ain't shit, now let's go where da real hoes at."

"Oh, NOW you wanna party?" Silky's voice got louder.

"Muafuckin right ahm gone party, shidd, you ain't?"

Silky opened his mouth to respond but upon thinking twice decided not to speak. This dispute would solve nothing and besides, the damage was done. Since it was near midnight they still had two hours to fool around at the club. Taking the 580 freeway to High Street, Silky exited and headed for their favorite hangout.

BUSINESS BEFORE PLEASURE

"Honey, I'll be back in a minute," Shakey told his woman.

"Umm ... where you goin?" Sheila asked drowsily.

"Ahm goin ta see how Yolanda's holdin up."

He had already taken a shower and dressed. Kissing Sheila softly on the cheek, Shakey turned and walked out. Casually strolling the narrow walkway to the other side of the third floor, he stopped at Yolanda's door and rang the bell. There was no answer so he tried again.

Realizing no one was home, Shakey turned and went back to Sheila's place. Since it was nearing noon, he decided to grab a bite to eat then go back to the police station and register with the identification unit.

"Hey honey, I'll be back in a few hours," he said.

"OK baby," she replied. "What do you want for dinner?"

"Jus yo love, gurlll ... ," he clowned.

"You got that, baby," she said while stretching.

Shakey kissed her mouth with force, causing his manhood to swell up. He considered undressing and taking her long lean body right then but knew if he did, all business would be cancelled until tomorrow. Rising up off the bed, he bounced.

Since Sheila was assigned only one stall inside the court's parking lot, Shakey's hoopty sat on West Grand Avenue. He got in his Caddy, a royal-blue '83 Coupe de Ville, and started the engine. Looking up, he noticed a parking ticket on his windshield.

"I'll be a muthafucka," he spoke to himself.

Getting back into his ride, he studied the ticket and realized it was given because his car was parked during street sweeping hours. Since he was in jail and couldn't possibly move it, he laughed while cruising off. The first stop he made was at Burrito Villa.

Located on Market Street two blocks from the court, Burrito Villa was a tiny Mexican stand that served all orders to go. The prices were cheap, servings large, and the food was on hits. Shakey pulled into the lot and winced at all the teenagers on lunch break from McClymond's High School waiting to order.

The owner was a middle-aged Latino who worked alone. No matter how fast he prepared meals, the line continued to move at a snail's pace. The guy seemed to know everyone by first name, and the kids didn't mind the wait.

Shakey stood at the back amused by the conversation going on amongst the teenyboppers. The girls were talking about the boys, the boys talking about the girls, and the jocks were engaged in rap about sports. Many of the girls were fully developed, causing Shakey's brain to consider riding a few.

The boys had their pants hanging down their butts, proudly displaying boxer shorts, which he found disgusting. Shakey knew that if they were in prison, they would not make their booty so easily accessible. Most of the kids whispered to each other about Shakey while avoiding eye contact. Many in the crowd knew of his reputation but everyone ignored him.

After twenty minutes he eased up to the counter window and ordered a beef soft taco along with a root beer soda. The taco cost a dollar and a half but was wrapped like and resembled a large burrito. The price for this item should have been three bucks considering the size of it.

Shakey paid the man, retrieved his food, then ate on the spot while leaning against his ride. Once he had consumed his meal and quenched his thirst, he got in his Caddy and rolled. Deciding to drive through town, he hooked a left on Market, rode West Grand to Broadway, and made a right.

The lunchtime crowd was out in full force, and Shakey got more than an eyefull. He cruised slowly, twisting his neck, honking, and shouting obscenities to the many beautiful women heading back to their jobs. Pulling up a block away from OPD, he parked, filled the meter with coins, and strutted into the station without a care in the world.

Taking the elevator to the third floor, he entered room 313. Getting in line, he waited his turn.

"May I help you, sir?" the lady asked.

"Yes, I'm here to register."

"Do you have an appointment?"

"Yes." He gave her his papers.

"Have you ever registered in Alameda County?" she asked.

"No, I haven't."

"What are you registering for?"

"Drugs."

"OK, the process takes two hours...."

"Two hours!" he interrupted, "jus ta be fanga-printed?"

"Yes, two hours. Now after you're processed, you don't have to wait here. We have a cafeteria in the basement or you can leave and come back, but you must get here before we close at four or you'll have to come back and re-register."

"OK, I'll do it now and get it out the way."

"Fill out this form, please."

She gave Shakey the registration form then went to her computer to pull up his rap sheet. The monitor displayed his drug charge, along with the charge of domestic violence. The ID tech, a nice-looking sister named Roxie, glanced at Shakey then shook her head in disgust because she, like most females, despised women beaters.

Shakey looked up from the counter and noticed one of Roxie's co-workers typing at a desk.

"Hello Earlene," he cracked.

"Excuse me," she responded.

"I said 'hello Earlene'."

"Do we know each other?" she questioned.

"Not the way we 'sposed to," he joked.

"Sir, I think you have me mistaken for someone else."
She went to view his criminal activity file on the monitor.

"You don't remember, do you?" he asked.

"Remember what?" She spoke firmly.

"Ah'm the one who was in here last week."

"Now look," she stared at his rap sheet before turning
to him, "what exactly are you in here for?" Her tone was
angry.

"A trumped-up drug charge."

"That's it," she demanded.

"Naw, dat ain't it but dare's two sides to each story."

"Candace!" she called out to another employee.

"What is it, Earlene?" Candace asked, coming out of
the print room.

"Will you and Roxie register this client, please?" she
said while storming off into the boss' office.

"I got it, girl — take a break," Candace told her friend.

Earlene plopped down into a chair then through clenched
teeth explained the situation to her supervisor.

"Andrew, you need to talk to that fool."

"What fool?" he said while momentarily looking up
from his computer monitor.

"The damn wife-beater out there who's harassing me."

"Hold your seat," he said as he got up.

Andrew Gordon was a blond-haired, handsome white
guy who knew that Earlene Johnson didn't play. He also
knew that if he didn't control the situation, she would.
Earlene was from the streets and when pushed into a corner, she didn't hesitate to "bring out the ghetto," as proven
on occasion.

Shakey was attempting to fill out his form at the counter

but needed help because he could neither read, write, nor spell too well. When he looked up for Candace's assistance, he found himself staring directly into the eyes of a barrel-chested white dude.

"What's the problem, sir?" asked Andrew.

"Ah need help wit dese papers," Shakey answered.

"Look, sir, you cannot come in here harassing my employees," Andrew said firmly.

"Man, I ain't harassed nobody."

"What do you call it then?"

"Ah jus gave the woman a compliment," Shakey mumbled.

"OK, sir," Andrew said as he continued to stare him down, "any more complaints about your compliments and I'll have to ask you to leave, understand?"

"Ah git yo drift, pahtna." Shakey growled.

"Sir, I'm not your partner," Andrew concluded then walked off. Entering his office again, he said, "OK Earlene, take a break."

"I'm fine," she returned, "I just wanted you to be aware of a possible situation." Rising from her seat, she walked out.

Andrew resumed his paperwork duties on the computer, not noticing that Earlene made a beeline towards Shakey.

"You need help with the form?" she asked softly.

"Yeah, ah do," he answered, surprised that she would assist him.

The next ten minutes were spent with Earlene making Shakey feel like an idiot because of his lack of penmanship. Instead of asking him questions then filling out the form, she watched him misspell words, corrected him, used White-Out to mask his mistakes, and made him try again. The ghetto in her was in full effect.

Secretly, she wrote down each answer he provided on a blank form. Once she was finished showing him how stupid he was, she told him, "Sign here, please."

Shakey signed the dotted line and turned to find a seat when Earlene blurted out, "Oh, I need you to sign this form too."

He didn't even look at it, just signed as instructed. If he had, he would have known that he signed the same form twice — one full of White-Out, and one mistake-free. Earlene gave Roxie and Candace the "eye," then laughed all the way to the print room. She'd gotten even.

Shakey sat down and patiently waited for his name to be called. He understood the change in Earlene. She had to prove to him that she was from the same ghetto streets as he, therefore, she rose above the incident and tried to make him look like a fool instead.

The waiting area was full as usual with people needing to be fingerprinted for employment purposes. Others would be sent by the judge for prints, then return across the street to the courthouse for their sentence. Some waited to view the sex offender computer file in order to find out if their neighbor was a pervert, but the majority were there for the same reason as Shakey: to register.

Registration was required so the police would know you were out of jail and where they could locate you. Shakey used Nadine's address even though she was dead.

He knew that if Five-O found out that his legal address was his mom's house in Richmond, or that the actual bed he slept in was at Sheila's, they could arrest him on the spot.

This was a risk he didn't mind taking because he didn't want to go all the way to Richmond just to be finger-printed and photographed, nor was he about to give out Sheila's address so Five-O could harass him whenever they were in the neighborhood.

"Calvin Jones," Candace called out.

Shakey went into the print room and stood waiting for instructions just inside the door. The print room was tiny but served its purpose as one of the most important areas of the police station. There was an old desk and a large Identex machine used for electronic fingerprinting. This machine resembled a stacked washer/dryer unit, with the dryer portion being the computer monitor.

A six-foot wood bench lined the wall to the right of the fake washer/dryer; it was where registrants placed their purse, backpacks, jackets, or children. To the left was a countertop with old-fashioned printing equipment (inkpad and roller). Next to that was a large trash barrel and a sink for washing up.

In the center of the room sat a bolted-down tripod holding a very outdated camera. A barber's chair without the leg or armrests was situated directly in front of that monstrosity.

"Step over here, please." Candace pointed to the chair while flicking on an overhead lamp.

Shakey sat down in the chair and "mean mugged" for

the camera as Candace flicked the photo. When she turned around to shut off the lamp, he ogled her big booty.

"Now, step to the machine, please," she asked.

Shakey stepped to the washer/dryer and proceeded to be electronically printed. This function was the main reason for the two-hour wait because the information was relayed to the state. Once received, it was checked by the state, passed on to the county, then returned to the city.

After getting an old-fashioned print job with ink on paper, Shakey waited for further instructions.

"OK, there will be a two-hour wait, so you can leave and come back, or wait in the next room. If you leave, make sure you return before we close at four or you'll have to go through the entire process again." Candace's warning was matter-of-fact.

"I'll be back," Shakey said then walked out.

During the entire booking process for Shakey, Earlene would bring in paperwork for other clients, never failing to laugh at Shakey behind his back. Her head was held high.

"Girl, what if he's late and has to start over tomorrow?" Earlene asked.

"Then Roxie will get her turn," Candace said as all three women laughed loudly.

6
now you know

Silky and Junebug rolled up to the Screamin Eagle and got out of the Mongoose. Happy faces greeted their arrival as if they were stars. This was Junebug's environment — being a big fish in a small pond. Silky acted natural, like this sort of praise was supposed to occur.

"The Eagle," as it was dubbed, was a bonafide hole in the wall. Nothing more than a neighborhood club, it was a clay and brick building that outwardly resembled a warehouse more than a nightspot.

The bouncer at the door was a brother named Marv who stood six feet four and weighed a hefty three hundred pounds. He was wearing black slacks and shoes, along with a yellow and black dashiki. High yellow, he had a four-inch-thick afro with bushy sideburns connected to his full-grown beard and mustache.

"Marv baby, I thought you'd be happy to see us," Junebug blurted out while displaying all thirty-two.

Marv's eyes remained deadpan as he scanned both dudes with his hand-held metal detector. The dude didn't play and everyone knew it. Junebug considered himself above everyone else, so he thought he could get away with clowning Marv.

"Five-dollar cover charge," Marv boomed.

"Silky, pay da man," Bug said as he entered, only to be stopped by Brick.

Brick was Marv's longtime partner, and his temper was shorter. He stood six-three, weighing in at a powerful two-seventy-five. He sported a low-to-the-scalp natural, clean-shaven face, gray tank top, brown leather weightlifter's belt, gray sweatpants, and white hi-top sneakers.

His demeanor was serious, and when he motioned for Junebug to spread 'em, there was no clowning. Brick patted down Junebug and Silky, then allowed them to enter. He and Marv would exercise this routine hundreds of times before the night was over and no one would resist.

No one would act up inside either, because those two had a reputation for inflicting serious bodily harm. It was nothing for them to throw a fool across a table before punching his lights out and tossing him out of the joint by the seat of his pants.

The inside of the club was much larger than one would expect. There was a carpeted seating area with ten square tables and four chairs around each one. A fifty-two-inch television screen sat in the far right-hand corner showing music videos without the volume.

An entry door leading to the restrooms was situated right beneath the screen, with pinball machines on either side. The bar spanned the distance with fifteen stools in front of it. Manning the bar was a sister named Melody who was both sharp-tongued and sexy.

Directly behind her was a row of evenly spaced wood columns, which served to split the club in two. The far side housed another carpeted seating area for seventy-five, a small twelve-by-twelve dance floor, and an elevated DJ booth. As usual, the club was filled to capacity.

"Well, if it ain't God's gift to women!" Melody shouted as she spotted Silky greeting everyone in the place.

"Thank you," he said while walking over to her.

The bar patrons parted like the Red Sea as Silky took on the role of kingpin. Melody wore a leopard-design leotard one-piece that appeared to be painted on. Her complexion was cocoa-butter brown and her body was sculpted. She was a brick shithouse even at forty, and would age gracefully.

Her hair was a gold-dyed curl, and she displayed curves in all the right places. With gold rings, ropes, long fingernails, and nose ring, she looked sassy.

"Silky Johnson, I ain't seen you in weeks. What's her name?"

"Monae," Silky hollered.

"Monae?" Melody continued, "Monae what?"

"Monae Green."

"Well, when are we going to meet Ms. Monae Green?"

"You can meet her right now," he smiled.

"OK, go get her."

Silky reached into his pocket and pulled out a folded wad of cash held in place by a rubber band. Peeling off three one-hundred-dollar bills, he shouted.

"Drinks for the house, compliments of Monae Green."

"Boy, you ain't shit, niggah!" Melody said while happily filling orders.

"Melody, if you ever take a minute to know me, I guarantee you'll stop calling me 'boy'."

"Give me a hug, you fool."

Silky leaned over the bar and hugged Melody's upper torso. She hugged back but before she released the embrace, he kissed her temple, which sent a chill through her body.

"Alright now," she laughed, "you know I don't want your mama coming down here accusing me of robbing the cradle."

"If Mama came here she'd meet the future Mrs. Johnson," he boasted.

"Silky, you know I'm old enough to be yo mama."

"And that's what I'd call you, MAMA."

The crowd roared its approval at his comeback line as he walked away. Melody stood there blushing in amazement at the fine young man Silky had become. Forty years old, she'd known him since he was a child, but there was something about him that separated him from the rest.

Melody was intrigued and fascinated by Silky. For the remainder of the evening, she would steal glances at him while pouring drinks, only to be ignored. This piqued her interest even more, because most men would spend the entire night at the bar trying to talk her out of some snatch.

Silky was different and she understood it. He had business to conduct and a performance to put on. He walked over to a table occupied by two beautiful Nubian queens and sat down. They had witnessed the entire scene at the bar and were still giggling.

"What's up, Tash?" he spoke.

"Nothing but the rent Silky. Meet my friend Renee."

"Hello, Renee." Silky kissed the back of her hand.

"Hi," she said meekly while grinning.

"I see 'Bug is at his usual best," Tasha stated.

They all looked in Junebug's direction and laughed as they watched him rapping to a stoutly built, ugly welfare broad.

"Yeah, he done lowered himself to the blind, crippled, and crazy," Silky whispered.

Tasha and Renee broke out in laughter as Silky motioned for a waitress. The cocktail server strutted to the table instantly, giving Silky his props.

"Silky Johnson, just as fine as ever," she said.

"Hello Sheena, I think you know Tasha, this is Renee," Silky returned.

"Hi y'all, what'll it be?"

"Bring us a bottle of champagne, Sheena."

"OK, Silky."

Sheena ignored all the other customers and made a beeline for the bar. Silky was a known big tipper, and since tips produced more income than salary, she would not make him wait. Sheena was average-looking with sagging tits, but her legs were mouth-watering. They were long and athletic, made for sex. Silky returned his focus to Tasha then asked, "Everythang alright?"

"It's a piece of cake, dude," she answered.

Tasha was big-boned with a caramel complexion and pearl-white teeth. She wore a natural hairdo cut three inches from the scalp, along with oval earrings and dark lipstick. Painted-on black jeans revealed wide hips and a huge behind; big breasts spilled out of a skimpy white halter top. Dark polished, neatly manicured nails jutted out from her opened-toed black high heels.

She had been a drug runner for Silky for the past two years and was good at it. Silky had several women on his crew because he realized they were extremely proficient at moving product. Since Tasha had a new girl with her and didn't give him a signal not to discuss business, he considered Renee a possible recruit. Slapping a c-note on the table, he told Tasha, "Pay Sheena for the drink and I'll be back in a little while, OK honey?"

"You got it, bossman," Tasha replied.

Silky got up and headed for the restroom. After a few minutes he reappeared, greeting everyone he knew at tables and standing. They were treating Silky like a giant. Melody continued to steal glances from the bar while Silky ignored her, even though he did peep her game. He had her right where he wanted and would cap on it later.

Strolling to the DJ's booth amid handshakes and pats on the back, Silky was the man.

"Silky Johnson in the house!" blurted "Baby Blow" over the sound system.

"Baby Blow, how ya doin?" Silky said as he made his way into the booth.

"Whatup boyyyy?" Baby Blow said grinning as they embraced.

Baby Blow was decked out in white slacks, shoes, rayon shirt, and Kangol brim. He was a handsome thirty-year-old who held a striking resemblance to Blair Underwood. He and Silky engaged in small talk before Silky exited the booth and continued his rounds. Stopping at Junebug, who was busy making rounds of his own, they rapped.

"'Bug, I see you in yo element, huh?"

"You damn right, Silk, dis mah goddamn turf," he boasted.

"What time you gone be ready to raise, dude?"

"When da club close, man, shidd!" Junebug laughed at his own response.

"Awight, we leave at two," Silky stated.

"Cool," Junebug returned.

Silky rejoined Tasha and Renee and proceeded to give a toast. As usual, he drank soda. Renee wore blue jeans and red heels with a red leotard top. Her permed black hair hung down to her shoulders with curls at the bottom. She had big lips, a beautiful midnight-black face, and looked like she had a phine body, although Silky couldn't tell because she was sitting.

"I make a toast to my girl Tash and her gorgeous new friend Renee," Silky said as he hoisted his glass.

"I'll testify to that shit," Tasha co-signed.

"Thank you," Renee blushed as she clinked glasses with them.

The ladies spent the next hour laughing and being entertained by Silky's wit and charm. Once Baby Blow crooned, "Last dance, y'all," the threesome rose to leave. Silky stuffed a fifty-dollar bill down Sheena's bra and she gave him a non-verbal response as if to say, "If you want me, you got me." He smiled at her google eyes and walked out arm in arm with the girls.

The crowd filed out of the club but failed to disperse. People lingered in front of the building socializing, trying to get seven digits, or just hanging out not ready to go home. The cool night air was filled with the aroma of weed as joints were fired up everywhere.

Fools peeled rubber pulling off, while others attempted donuts in the intersection. They didn't seem to care that one slip of the hand on the steering wheel would result in a major catastrophe — to them this stupidity was fun.

Many of the onlookers laughed loudly and praised the foolishness, while others urinated on homes, cars, or wherever they chose to relieve themselves. This after-party activity is what riled neighborhood residents the most. Every weekend they would wake up in the morning having to clean their property of litter, broken glass, and drug paraphernalia, not to mention facing a street covered with black skid marks.

Silky stood in the middle of the pack rapping with Tasha and Renee. Marv locked the club's doors, meaning everyone was on their own. Tasha slid Silky a wad of cash with the unspoken understanding between the two that he would deliver a fresh package in the morning.

Amongst the chaos, no one seemed to notice the black Chevy slowly rolling down the block with its lights turned off. Silky saw a figure lean out the window, which he immediately recognized as Skye. Looking directly at the muzzle of the gat, he ducked for cover.

Skye opened fire while the throng of partygoers shot off in all directions. Renee took a bullet to the heart and was dead before her head slammed on the dirty pavement. Tasha screamed loudly from the gut and furiously attempted CPR.

Lou hooked a left at the next corner, then passed the joint of weed to Skye.

"Think you hit 'im?"

"Naw Lou, but now he know his ass in trouble," Skye answered.

"You see dose fools duckin for cover?" Lou grinned.

"Yeah boy, but dat's only da beginnin — I'mo kill Silky's ass," Skye stated matter-of-factly.

Lou headed for Da Spot as Skye reclined in his seat hitting the weed. He didn't get his man, but now at least Silky knew he was marked. Skye was happy.

7
THE INVESTIGATION

Within minutes of the shooting, the street was swarmed with squad cars, ambulances, news media, and evidence technicians. By the time homicide detectives arrived, the front of the club had been cordoned off with yellow tape which shouted "CRIME SCENE – DO NOT ENTER." A small crowd of neighborhood residents gathered at the corner viewing what they considered a disgusting sight. Monday morning they would again be at City Hall demanding that this nightspot be permanently closed.

Employees from the coroner's office zipped up Renee's lifeless figure in a body bag and sped off to do their job. Three other people were shot in the drive-by, but their injuries were minor. They were transported by ambulance to local hospitals to be treated and released. The police would question them later, but of course, they couldn't help because they were innocent bystanders.

Since Tasha was crying uncontrollably and it was obvious that she and Renee were friends, the police escorted her back inside the club. Silky, Junebug, and his new skeezer "Peaches" went inside too.

Marv, Brick, and Sheena, along with the rest of the cocktail waitresses, sat at tables twiddling their thumbs. They knew nothing, but Five-O would not allow them to leave until the evidence techs completed taking their photos of the murder scene.

Baby Blow packed his records while Melody busily tidied up her work station. The owner, a fat fifty-something-year-old guy named Ollie, nervously paced the floor. He knew this after-party activity was bad for business and that his club would be blamed for the night's events. The thought never crossed his mind that a young lady had been killed right outside his establishment; he was thinking damage control.

The detectives stood off to the side gathering all data from uniformed patrol officers before heading to the table where the bouncers and waitresses sat.

"You guys can leave but it will be one at a time," Detective Johnson boomed before walking away.

Marv was the last one to go, and when the steel door slammed behind him Detective Johnson focused his attention on Tasha, making a beeline to her table. Nathan Johnson was the senior homicide detective for OPD. Standing six feet six inches on a powerfully built three-hundred-pound frame, he towered over the table.

Johnson had been with the force for almost twenty years and was relentless when it came to solving murders. He had a knack that came naturally because he left no clue unchecked. Graying at the temples and rapidly approaching fifty, Johnson possessed an air of authority. He wore an outdated blue suit with a plain tie, black shoes, low-cut afro, and wedding band on his ring finger.

"Ma'am, I'd like to ask you a few questions," he said to Tasha.

"OK," she whispered meekly.

"Follow me," he ordered.

"Officer, I have a question!" Junebug stated, trying his best to appear sober.

"And you are. . . ?" Johnson arched his brow.

"Anthony Grimes."

"What is it?"

"I was wondering if my lady and me could leave too."

"As long as she drives."

"I wouldn't have it any other way," said Junebug while rising up from his chair. "Dude, I'll get with you later," he told Silky.

Johnson led Tasha to a table in the far corner and pulled out a chair for her to sit. Manny Hernandez, his partner, jotted down the name, address, and phone number of Peaches and Junebug before allowing them to leave. He had done this routine with every person in the club.

Silky looked up and saw Hernandez heading his way.

"Hello sir, I'm Sergeant Hernandez and I need to know if you can tell me anything you may have seen or heard."

"Once I heard the first shot, I ducked for cover."

"So you're saying you didn't see anything."

"Correct."

"Did you know the victim?"

"We just met tonight."

"Did you see the suspects?"

"No, I didn't," Silky calmly stated.

"How about the car?"

"I was ducking for my safety, so I really didn't see anything."

"OK, I'll need to get your name, address, and phone number for my records."

Hernandez wrote down the information Silky provided then joined Johnson and Tasha at their table, only he remained standing. Manny Hernandez never sat down while on a case. Tonight he wore a standard gray suit, white shirt, burgundy tie, and black shoes. He had both the look and demeanor of a cop.

Standing five feet eight inches short with slick black hair combed backwards, Manny was proud of his Mexican heritage. He couldn't understand why many in his community considered him a sellout just because he enforced the law without compromise.

"Excuse me, Ms. Savoy," Johnson said to Tasha.

He and Hernandez walked to another corner and began talking in hushed tones. Silky joined Tasha at her table.

"How you feel, baby?"

"I'm OK, Silky."

"What did you tell him?"

"Nothing."

"Good," he said. "We'll get that bastard our own way."

"Muthafuckin right," Tasha growled.

"You guys OK?" Melody asked while heading their way.

"We're fine," Tasha answered.

"Silky, do you need anything before I call a cab?"

"A cab?" he answered her question with a question.

"Yes, that lemon of a car I have broke down again."

"You don't need a cab, baby, I'll give you a ride," Silky told her. "What about you, Tasha?"

"My car's outside."

"You cool with driving?" He was concerned.

"I'll be alright," she said.

"Let me get my things together," Melody said while walking away.

Johnson and Hernandez returned to the table where Silky and Tasha sat solemnly.

"Here's my card." Johnson handed one to each of them. "Call me if you remember anything, no matter how insignificant it may seem."

"OK," they said in unison.

"You guys are free to go." He shook their hands and stood watching as they walked out of the club with Melody.

Silky let Melody into the Mongoose then walked Tasha to her ride. It was late and they were tired so he hugged her, then spoke.

"You'll get your package tomorrow, then I'll take care of Skye."

"Silky, I want his ass."

"Baby, we both do, but you just go and get some rest, alright?"

"OK," she said then hugged him again.

"When you get home leave me a voicemail message so I'll know you're safe."

Tasha shook her head in agreement, got in her car, and

drove off. Silky went over to the Mongoose and casually slid in the driver's seat. Pulling off slowly, he turned on the beat and cruised to Melody's home.

Johnson and Hernandez finished their rap with fat Ollie, then walked out into the cool night air. Ollie huffed and puffed before finally securing the super-sized master lock into the slot. Turning around, he attempted to foot scrub out the chalk line, without success. Stogie dangling from his mouth, fat Ollie got into his Mercedes and rolled off.

Johnson opened the door to their unmarked police vehicle when, just before getting in, he noticed a curtain draw back from an apartment right across the street. The place was dark, but Johnson swore he saw the curtain move.

"Hold up, Manny, we have what may be our first eyewitness," he said while jaywalking over to the building.

Johnson located the manager's buzzer and mashed. Hernandez drew his service revolver from its holster, stepped to the side, and waited. The building's outer appearance was just like the rest on the block — storefront downstairs, single-family units up. It was ancient. A voice spoke over the intercom.

"Yesssss." It came from an elderly man.

"Police!" Johnson spoke with authority. "Could you let us in?"

"Awight, let me come open da doe . . . da buzzah don't work right."

The receiver went dead as Johnson pulled his badge from his belt clip. An elderly man shuffled down the stairs wearing a black housecoat, slippers, and tube socks to the knees. He held a large coffee can. He peered through the see-through curtains at Johnson's badge. Johnson saw him first but acted like he didn't.

"Yaw da poe-leese," the man stated slowly.

"Yes sir, I'm Johnson and this is my partner Hernandez." He put away his badge.

"What yaw wont?"

"We're investigating a murder across the street, and you are...?"

"Da name's Bobby Reese, but 'ehbody call me Uncle Bob." He spat a gob of snuff into the can.

"Well Uncle Bob, I need to ask you to step out for a moment and tell me who stays in that upstairs unit," Johnson pointed.

"Show me da one you pointin at."

Uncle Bob stepped out the door while placing balled-up tissue paper in it so it wouldn't lock. Looking up to where Johnson pointed, he casually stated, "Dass mah house."

"Good, then you're who I need to talk to."

"Man, what you need ta talk ta me foe?"

"Sir, there was a murder tonight at the club and I think you saw something."

"Ah ain't seed shit."

Johnson realized he had to change his strategy with the old man.

"Can we go inside?" he asked.

"Yaw follow me," Uncle Bob answered.

The threesome walked up the steps to Reese's flat and went inside. Uncle Bob closed the door and offered the two cops a seat. They both chose to stand because the inside of his home was filthy. Johnson spotted the window along with a chair off to the side. He knew he had his man. Hernandez felt his partner was onto something but didn't know what — he'd play it by ear.

"Mr. Reese," Johnson began, "I need to know how long have you been sitting at this window?" He felt the chair, noticing it was still warm.

"Long time, couple a hours."

"So you witnessed the shooting."

"Like ah tole yaw outside, ah ain't seed shit."

"Do you have children?"

"Yessss, why you ax me dat?"

"Because sir, if one of your children were murdered, wouldn't you want someone to tell what they knew about it?" Johnson laid on the guilt trip heavy.

"Ah reckon you right, but ah don't wont no trouble — dose young kids don't care 'bout nuttin."

"Sir, you have my word no harm will come to you. All the information you give us will be kept in the strictest of confidentiality."

"I'ont know...." Reese scratched his frail leg. "Ah needs time ta thank."

"OK, but you must remember, time is of the essence. The perpetrator has killed once and will kill again — let's hope the next one is not one of your children."

"All ah seed was da cah," Reese whispered.

"What kind of car was it?" Johnson pressed.

"I'ont know, it was black, dough."

"How many doors?"

"A foe-doe."

"Could you make out the model?"

"Looked lack a Chevy, matter uh fact, dass what it was, uh Chevy." Reese grinned then continued, "ah 'member 'cause ah used ta have one uh dose."

"Could you make out the license plate number?"

"Naw, it didn't have one, plus da lights was turned off."

"How many people were in it?"

"It was two of 'em — one drove while da other shot."

Johnson eyed his partner, who was busy writing down all the information. Nodding his head to Manny that they had gotten all Mr. Reese could give, they prepared to leave.

"Sir, here's my card." He handed his business card to Uncle Bob. "If you think of anything else, don't hesitate to call me, OK?"

"OK, suh," Uncle Bob responded.

Manny jotted down Reese's address and phone number, then he and Nate left. Jaywalking back across the empty street, they got in their car and headed for the station.

"Nate, I gotta hand it to ya, that was an excellent piece of police work," Manny stated.

"Thanks partner, let's grab something to eat on our way to headquarters."

"You got it, amigo, how about some burgers?"

"Burgers will be fine, Manny."

Tired from working overtime the last two weeks, they stopped to get burgers then headed for the office. After eating, they went to Renee's house to inform her folks of her death. Of all the assignments in police work, Johnson hated this one the most because this was where he found no proper way to tell someone that their loved one was dead. Renee's family would be no different.

Uncle Bob heard a knock at his door, and thinking it was the police again, opened it. His eyes grew big as saucers as he saw the large knife plunge into his chest. The killer pulled the knife out of his prone body and exited the building swiftly. Bobby Reese would tell no more.

8

MAH PAHTNA

Big Ed smiled through the glass window, sat down in the chair provided, then picked up the telephone receiver. He was more than happy to have a visitor.

"Whatup homes?" he greeted.

"Same ol, same ol," answered Skye. "How you be?"

"Jus makin da best of a bad situation."

"Know das right."

Skye and Big Ed chatted freely for a few minutes about nothing in particular. Skye was anxious to tell his boss that the operation was running smoothly but knew he would have to play it off, just in case the sheriffs were listening in on the conversation. Since Big Ed had been transported to Santa Rita Jail to await his court date, he had no clue as to what was going on in the streets of Oaktown.

Santa Rita is located off highway 580 just outside of Pleasanton, which is famous for hosting the yearly county fair. The jail is a rickety wood structure that resembles beat-up horse stables. Housing criminals from throughout Alameda County, this institution is transitional. Convicts serve short-term sentences, wait to be shipped to major penitentiaries, or are held at Santa Rita Jail until their court dates. Big Ed was in the latter group. Speaking in code, he resumed the conversation with questions about his kids and wife.

"Dude, witup isnup whiznit miznah kiznids?"

"Kiznids are fiznine, Shiznerl isniz plizna'er hiznatin an shit, dough." Skye spoke rapidly.

"Whiznut a-biznout miznah bahzizness?"

"Isahm hizandlin isnit."

"Any problems?"

"Just whiznone, yo biznoy wiznonts ta be da biznoss."

Ed knew he meant Silky. "WHAT?" Ed screamed.

"Niggah tiznellin fiznolks diznet hisnee riznunnin thiznangs."

"Oh, so he thank he in charge now, huh?" Ed was angry.

"Diznude," Skye gestured, "isnah giznot diznat shiznit isnin contriznol."

Translation:

Big Ed: What's up with my kids?

Skye: Kids are fine, Shirley's player hating, though.

Big Ed: What about my business?

Skye: I'm handling it.

Big Ed: Any problems?

Skye: Just one, yo boy wanna be the boss.

Big Ed: WHAT?

Skye: Niggah tellin folks that he runnin thangs.

Big Ed: Oh, he thank he in charge now, huh?

Skye: I got that shit in control.

Big Ed thought for a minute about what he'd just heard. He assumed the worst, considering his wife Shirley was tripping and Silky was already trying to take over his rule. Shirley was still upset because Big Ed had left her for Vanessa, who ironically would be the state's star witness at his trial. They'd set her up in the witness protection program, so as far as Ed was concerned, Skye would have to find her, then kill her.

"Whiznut a-biznout da biznitch?" Ed meant Vanessa.

"Isnah giznot fiznolks isnonit, diznon't wiznurry, we giznone fiznind diznat hiznoe & hisnandle isnit." Skye was sure that it was only a matter of time before Vanessa Harris was six feet under.

Translation:

Big Ed: What about the bitch?

Skye: I got folks on it, don't worry, we gone find that hoe and handle it.

Big Ed was happy to hear Skye's confidence about eliminating the one person who could send him to prison for the next twenty years. He knew if anyone could locate the whore, it was Skye. He was also happy about the fact that during the entire ghetto slang conversation, the only name they'd used was Shirley's. Ed had no doubt that the sheriffs would play back the tape over and over until they decoded the verse, but without names spoken, they couldn't prove a thing.

"Heard through the grapevine that you had a rumble with Shakey?" Skye asked.

"Yeah, ah was 'bout ta beat his ass down when Five-O broke it up," Ed boasted.

"Man...," Skye whistled, "I wish I was there, I would have helped you kick that niggah's ass."

"Dig it! Look homes, handle yo bizness and tell all dem fools ta come visit. I ain't convicted yet."

"You got it, boss." Skye was proud of himself for being first.

"Oh yeah, put some funds on my book, man."

"You got it, dude."

Big Ed rose from his seat and placed a balled-up fist against the glass, failing to put the phone back in the cradle. Skye did the same thing, then turned and walked down the hallway. He wanted to tell Big Ed about the drive-by at the club last night but thought it would be too risky. Heading to the lobby, he stopped at the line to leave money on Big Ed's book but declined to wait after seeing thirty people in front of him.

He had to leave because Santa Rita gave him the creeps. Deciding instead to leave the money at North County tomorrow, he bounced. North County was right across the street from Oaktown's jail, and since Tuesday was store day at Santa Rita, Big Ed would neither know nor care that the money was deposited on Monday. Skye knew it didn't make a difference anyway.

Skye went to the parking lot, got in his ride, and drove off. His car was a black '76 Camaro, complete with humps on the hood and spoiler on the tail. It was customized and clean as a whistle, with the dashboard panel digitalized, a ground-shaking sound system, built-in sunroof, and shiny mag rims, along with deep-treaded tires.

Skye pulled off the prison grounds, then lit up a joint of weed. After hitting it, he let out a sound that resembled a stifled sneeze, coughed a few times, then hit it again. Blasting the beat, he rolled 580 back to the hood.

When he woke the next day it was past noon, his usual wakeup time. He got dressed then headed for North County to leave a hundred dollars on the books for Big Ed.

The county offices were connected to the city offices by a catwalk joining both buildings' second floors. Metal detector machines sat solemnly at each entrance, except the door leading to the money line and the first floor of the police station.

Skye knew he would not have to go through the detectors, but he left his hunting knife in his ride anyway, along with the loose change jingling in his pocket. He knew that once you entered the building the sheriff's deputies could search you for no reason, so he would play it safe.

He left the money on the books for Big Ed then went back to his car, which was parked in a handicapped spot displaying the fake placard he owned dangling from the mirror. Placing the key in the ignition, he started the engine, looked up to join traffic, then smiled. Shakey Jones was leaving police headquarters.

"I'mo follow dis fool," he said to himself.

Shakey got in his Caddy and took off like a bat out of hell. Skye didn't know why he was driving like a fool right in front of OPD and didn't care. All he knew was that

Shakey would not lose him. Shakey hit the 880 freeway with Skye running a red light in order not to lose sight of him. Following from a one-exit distance, he trailed his enemy to the probation department.

Stopping at the parking lot entrance, he watched Shakey go into the probation office. He parked his car right next to Shakey's, got out, then chose a hiding spot in the bushes.

"Got yo ass, niggah," Skye said to himself, then waited.

9
A MELODIC TUNE

"Would you like to come in for a minute?" Melody asked.

"How about me escorting you to your door?" Silky answered.

"That'll work."

Silky got out of the Mongoose, then walked around to Melody's door and opened it. She slid out, cupped her arm inside his crooked elbow, and led the way. Her place was located on Greenridge Drive, an L-shaped block off Mountain Boulevard, which sat at the foot of Oaktown's hills. The entire block consisted of high-rent apartments and was quiet.

Melody climbed the three flights of stairs with Silky following close behind. Gazing at her butt, he silently wondered if she wore a thong or no underwear at all. Her body suit displayed no panty line so all he saw was a delicious-looking booty.

"Silky? There's something about murder that scares me, especially with it happening right outside the club," she shivered.

"What do you think it is?" he rubbed her shoulders.

"I don't really know. It is spooky, though. I mean, who were they shooting at?"

"Honey, I can't call it, I was too busy ducking like everybody else," he lied.

"That just goes to show one minute you're here and the next you're gone. Well, I won't hold you up. Thanks for the ride, baby."

Melody kissed Silky lightly on the lips then placed her key in the lock when his pager began vibrating on his belt clip.

"Let me use your phone to check my message — it should be Tasha."

Melody opened the door and flicked on the light switch in one motion. Dropping her purse on the floor along with her keys, she spoke rapidly, "Phone's by the coffee table, honey — I have to use the restroom."

Silky closed the door, walked over to the phone, and dialed while standing. The message on his voicemail was just as he assumed, from Tasha. She was home. Satisfied, he returned the receiver to its holder. Glancing around, he was impressed. The furnishings were expensive and the crib was clean.

A black entertainment center housed her television, cable box, video player, and mini component set, along with family photos on top. Next to that on the floor sat a full-sized figurine of a Manx cat, which he mistakenly thought to be a panther. Silky sat down on the leather sofa, which let out a whoosh from his weight. That plus the matching loveseat were both comfy and elegant. Placing his keys on the coffee table, he realized that it, along with the end units, were custom-made wood replicas of Jamaica, the Bahamas, and Puerto Rico.

Exotic oil paintings adorned the walls, and the aroma from all the scented candles gave the house a personality. To say he was impressed would be an understatement. Melody returned from the restroom rubbing her neck.

"You look like you're tired," Silky stated.

"Honey, that ain't the half of it." She took off her ear and nose rings. "I need to jump in the shower. Is everything alright with Tasha?"

"Yes, she's home safe, where I should be going."

He rose up off the sofa, walked over to Melody, and began massaging her neck from behind. She let her head fall back while closing her eyes. As her body began gyrating in sync with his fingers, Silky got hard. The more he rubbed, the more aroused he became. Melody pirouetted on her toes to face him. Pulling his mouth to hers, she kissed him deeply, letting her tongue do its own dance in his mouth.

Silky gently massaged her tits through the spandex, causing her nipples to poke out like two high beams.

"I think mama wants something," he said while boring into her eyes.

"Still with that mama shit, huh?" she said as she rubbed his hairy chest.

"What mama wants, she always gets. Now what do mama want?"

"Mama want baby!" she whispered.

Without another word, Melody jerked the one-piece off her body and stood proud like a stallion on display to potential bidders. Silky snaked his tongue into her mouth, kissing her deeply, while she eagerly returned the passion. Melody pulled off his jacket, tossing it on the sofa as her fingers furiously unbuttoned his shirt. Silky broke off the kiss, took her by the hand, and led her to the bedroom.

Once there, he disrobed while she waited anxiously in bed. He joined her and began sensuously kissing her breasts. While Melody's body gyrated in rhythm, Silky stuck a finger in her love canal. This produced moisture, but not enough, so he added a second finger and began wiggling them around.

He reached the desired moistness and mounted. As he glided in slowly, Melody began whispering his name. Silky continued to take his time even though she tried to speed up the action. He was determined not to ejaculate too soon, so he had to be in charge of his hormones. The deeper he went, the louder she became, and when he finally went buck wild, she screamed.

Silky plowed into her with a fury that she'd never known, and all she could do was accept it. The only thing she could do was to hold on for dear life while he rocked her world. By the time he was done, she'd chosen him. Silky rolled over gasping for breath as Melody lavished kisses on his neck, shoulders, and face.

She began kissing him in the mouth, which caused him to stiffen again. Returning her to her original position, he entered, only this time she received just his mushroom-shaped head. Silky plunged the mushroom in and out with rapid-fire precision, causing Melody to become delirious. They made love off and on for the rest of the night and most of the next day. Taking a shower together, Melody spoke.

"Will you drop me off for work, honey?"

"Yes," he said while penetrating from behind.

"Will you p-p-pick me UP?" she yelled as he banged away.

"What you thank?" he asked while depositing another load of cream into what was now his bank account.

"I think you will," she giggled.

Silky dropped Melody off at the club then sped away. She went inside and began setting up the bar, but her mind was on her man and the beautiful sex she'd been given the last sixteen hours. Due to the murder, the club was quiet, Melody could not remember a Sunday night ever being this slow. The clock moved at a snail's pace as she sat on her stool behind the counter, bored to death.

Pulling the Mongoose into his assigned stall at the Jamaican Arms, Silky casually strolled to his crib. Once inside, he undressed and took another shower, liberally splashing on cologne, brushing his teeth, and rubbing himself down with baby oil. Since he had no plans and wanted some much-needed rest, he put on a burgundy warm-up suit. Going to the kitchen, he poured himself a large glass of lemonade then pushed the message button on his answering machine.

The messages were all generic — one each from Junebug, Tasha, his mom, and three from Neisha. Erasing them all, he figured he'd better wash his dirty clothes because there was no telling when he would be back once he picked up Melody. She was different from any woman he had ever met.

She didn't make him beg for booty — her sexual appetite was starving just like his, and she had tons of experience. He liked everything about that woman, and all woman she was.

The laundry room hours were from ten in the morning until ten at night, so since it was already eight, Silky knew he could only wash one of his two loads. He gathered up a bundle of colored clothing, along with seven quarters, and headed for the community wash house. The apartment units were not equipped with washer/dryer hookups, so all tenants had to use the facilities provided by the management.

The door was already open when he got to it, but the sight he saw caused him to nearly drop his basket. Bent over a washer, re-adjusting clothes, was the gray girl he'd peeped out at the pool the day before. She wore a short blue skirt, no shoes, bikini top, and if she had on underwear, it had to be a thong. Silky's manhood rose to full attention.

"I see we have a problem," he said by way of announcing his presence.

"The damn thing always tilts," she said without looking back.

"You need any help?" he asked.

"No, I'm fine," she answered.

"I have no doubts about that, but I was referring to the machine."

She stopped moving clothes and turned around to face her admirer, unable to avoid the large print in his sweatpants.

"You just moved here, right?" she asked.

"Yes, and from the looks of it, I'm staying!" They both laughed.

"Hi, my name is Bridgette." She extended a hand.

"Duane," he said, "but you can call me Silky." He held on longer than necessary.

"So do you normally wash at night?" she said.

"I do now," he smiled.

"Thank you!"

"No need, I just call it like I see it, and I see phine. Where's your man?" He got serious.

"My husband's home, snoring his brains out."

"I see, an early riser?"

"No, just drunk." She laughed at her own remark.

"How long you been married?"

"Two years."

"Happily?"

"Well, we have our differences," she said.

"What do you mean?" Silky pressed.

"Umm . . . he's kinda boring."

"Oh, he can't satisfy you." Silky was direct.

"Why do you say that?"

"Any time a woman says her man is boring, he can't fuck."

"And I assume you can?"

Silky, bold as he was, flicked the light switch off, pulled her to him, and thrust his tongue deep into her mouth. Bridgette had never considered having sex with a black man, so the kiss caught her totally off guard. At first she tried to break away, but his grip wouldn't allow it. As she felt his meat gyrating on her stomach, her resistance turned into passion. The thrill of being discovered making out with a Negro caused her body to take control of her mind.

Silky kissed her with urgency and she responded just as hungrily, her hips moving in rhythm with his. He felt underneath her skirt and was pleasantly surprised to find that she wasn't wearing panties. Jerking down his sweats, he located her hole with his finger, then plunged into her. The moment she felt his thick meat slide into her vagina, a soft moan escaped her lips, breaking off a beautiful kiss.

The position wasn't right even after he lifted up her right leg for a better angle, so he whispered in her ear.

"Bend over."

Bridgette placed her palms on the washer, spread her legs, and let Silky have his way. He began his sexual version of the cabbage patch, running man, and four corners. In the darkness of the laundry room, she bit her lip, shook her head from side to side, and clutched the washing machine like a vice grip. Try as she might to be silent, the girl was moaning constantly. She was enjoying this young black stud and knew he would be getting it whenever he wanted from now on.

Silky plowed into the fine piece of white meat as if there were no tomorrow. The harder he hit, the more she moaned. He knew they had started something dangerous but good. Once he relieved his pressure, he pulled out, flicked the light switch back on, then sat on the folding table admiring her statuesque frame.

Bridgette remained bent over gasping for breath. Grabbing a wet towel from the washer, she wiped herself clean then sat next to him.

"I'll leave my work number for you on your windshield — you can call me whenever you like, OK?" she asked.

"My memory is pretty good so just tell me what it is."

"Alright, and you tell me yours."

They gave each other the numbers verbally then she hugged him. Flicking the lights back off, she kissed him sensuously, not caring that his juice ran freely down her leg. Turning the lights back on she walked out smiling. Silky picked up his basket and went back home to take yet another shower, the front of his sweats stained with their juice. He wrote down her number, took his bath, and sprawled across the bed butt naked, dreaming about Bridgette.

At one a.m. his alarm clock rattled noisily, ruining his wonderful dream.

10
PAYBACK

Alameda County's probation office is located in the industrial part of town. The area is saturated with hi-tech companies, medical facilities, telemarketing firms, service stations, and assorted bank branches and credit unions. As Shakey strolled through the swinging doors, he was still stewing over Earlene's successful effort to make him look like a fool.

A young Latina female sat at the reception desk talking on the phone. "Mr. Jones, is it?" she asked.

"Oh, you remembered," he smiled.

"Let me call you back," she whispered into the mouthpiece and hung up the phone. "The boss called in sick today but said to tell you he'll see you first thing in the morning."

"You mean he ain't heah?" Shakey's voice got loud.

"Mr. Jones!" her voice remained calm.

"What!?" he hollered.

"Take a deep breath." He did as instructed. "Inhale . . . Hold it . . . Now exhale."

Shakey looked at her with a newfound respect because her breathing exercise worked. He was once again calm, realizing it wasn't her fault that her boss wasn't there.

"OK, let's try it again," she said softly. "I can schedule your appointment first thing in the morning — is that OK?"

"I guess I have no choice."

"We'll see you in the morning," she said. "Have a nice day."

"Yeah . . . right," he sighed as he turned to leave.

The young lady handed him an appointment card then wrote a memo to her boss. Rising up from her seat, she went down the hallway and placed the note in her supervisor's mailbox. The blue dress she wore hugged her fabulous frame and displayed an awesome pair of hairy muscular legs. When she turned around, Shakey's smiling face greeted her.

"It must be a recess in heaven," he flirted.

"What?" She looked curious.

"Must be a recess in heaven 'cause the number one angel's on Earth."

"I'll see you tomorrow, Mr. Jones."

"You sho will," he slowly wisecracked.

"Bye."

"Not goodbye, baby, it's moe like til we meet again."

"Get out of here!" she said smiling.

"Shidd, dat gurl likes yo ass boyyyyyyyyy," he spoke to his alter ego.

So full of himself that he was about to burst, Shakey strolled out the swinging doors like a rooster who'd just chosen a prized hen. After taking a few steps he felt a hand grab his mouth. He tried to defend himself but was too slow. The large hunting knife slit his throat from ear to ear. He clutched the wound with his hands in a futile attempt to stop the bleeding as the assassin placed a foot squarely on his behind and shoved him into the bushes.

Shakey felt leaves being poured over his body and tried to talk, but the only thing flowing was his own blood. He had always thought of himself as not afraid to die. Now with his life slowly slipping away, he was terrified. It seemed as though he were watching a slow-motion picture replaying his life. Flashing across his brain were images of his mother, children, ex-wife Cassandra, Sheila Rae, prison cells, and newspaper headlines describing his killing.

His body began to shake uncontrollably as the killer's footsteps got further away. Shakey attempted to get up one last time and rose slightly before dropping onto the dirt with a thud. He was dead.

Skye walked briskly back to his ride, lit up a blunt, and cruised off the lot. Big Ed would surely be glad to hear this piece of news. Feeling giddy about the day's work, Skye felt his stomach growl, reminding his brain that he had not eaten. Deciding on bar-b-que, he stopped at Flint's.

Located on the corner of 67th & East 14th, Flint's provides some of the best que in the city. The interior is small, with standing room for about ten people, so the line often snakes out the door onto the sidewalk. Skye stood in line inhaling the beautiful aroma of ribs, links, and chicken. The wait is never long, because the food is pre-cooked, so the staff only has to fix your order.

There was a stoutly built sister in front of him wearing blue jeans, tennis shoes, and a matching hooded sweat jacket. Her hair was styled in a short natural, and she had a big butt along with wide hips. Skye loved the view.

"I should have called in my order," he spoke.

"Me too," she said briefly, glancing back.

"Well, good as you look, I don't mind waiting."

"Thank you." She turned to face her admirer.

Not that it would have made any difference, Skye was pleased to see that baby had a pretty face and an even skin tone. Upon seeing his rugged mug, she stiffened.

"Honey, you look like you just seen a ghost, whatup wit dat?" Skye said.

"Nothing," the woman replied. "You just resemble someone I'm trying to forget."

"Well baby, like I always say, don't stereotype 'cause you may be wrong."

"Oh, is that what you say?" She loosened.

"Yes, that's what I say. My name's Skye — what's yours?"

"Is that what your parents named you?"

"No, but that's my name!"

"Hello Skye, my name's Tee."

"Oh, and yo parents named you dat?" he laughed.

"No, but that's what everybody calls me!" she laughed.

She continued facing Skye as they rapped, and he couldn't help but notice her large breasts, along with mushroom-sized nipples poking out. She wasn't wearing anything underneath her sweat jacket.

"Look honey, I ain't in no kinda rush, so why don't we get our food and eat together upstairs in the dining hall?" he asked.

"Why would I do that with a perfect stranger?" she answered his question with another.

"So we can get to know each other," he stated emphatically.

Looking him up and down, she finally responded.

"OK, I'll have lunch with you, Mr. Skye."

"Dare it is," he said like a mack, snapping his fingers for emphasis.

They ordered their meals, with Skye footing the bill. Tee put her money back into her purse then headed up the stairs with Skye following closely behind. The dining room sat no more than forty people and consisted of ten square tables with four chairs each. Considering that most bar-b-que spots only have a few barstools lined up along the counters, Skye acted as though this were a five-star restaurant.

He pulled out a chair and nudged it while she sat, said a silent prayer before he ate, and for the majority of lunch, ate with his left hand under the table. Normally, both of his elbows would be on the table, hands greasy, and he'd lick his fingers without shame, showing no home training.

Today, Skye Barnes could have won an Academy Award
for his performance of manners.

"When we gone go out?" he asked.

"When do you want to?" she answered while devour-
ing a fork full of greens.

"Tonight sounds good to me."

"On a Monday, where would we go?" she asked incred-
ulously.

"Lots of places. They got Monday Night Football
jumpin off at all the clubs, then the party starts after the
game. We could go to the movies, skatin, bowlin, you
name it and we'll go!"

"How about you give me your phone number, I meet
you at eight, then we decide," she said.

"That'll work. Give me a pen and some paper."

Tee handed Skye the writing tools and finished her
meal while he wrote down his address and phone number. He also jotted down his pager and cell phone numbers
to make sure she could reach him.

"OK baby, now let's seal the deal with a kiss," he said
while handing her the note.

She leaned across the table and softly kissed his lips
then rose up and walked back down the stairs. As soon as
she was out of sight, Skye wolfed down his food like a
man starving, then ate the remaining portion of links from
her plate. Stuffed and satisfied, he left without bothering
to leave a tip.

11
BAD CHAIN
OF EVENTS

Johnson and Hernandez reported for work on Sunday, which was normally their day off, and were met at the door by the new head of homicide, Edgar Lewis. Well-liked throughout the department, Lewis was a pleasant upgrade from Deputy Chief Spitz, their former boss. A proud black man, Edgar Lewis stood six feet two inches on a lean but powerful frame.

"Hello, guys." He shook their hands.

"Edgar, welcome aboard," Johnson smiled.

"Well, I hate to start the day off with bad news but I have no choice."

"What's up?" asked Hernandez.

"Found a dead body one hour ago. The victim's daughter was worried because he didn't call her this morning, which was his Sunday custom. Since he didn't answer her calls, she went to his place to check it out. Found him stabbed to death."

"What's the victim's name?" Hernandez inquired.

"Old guy named Bobby Reese."

"Reese!" Johnson boomed. "We just questioned him last night."

"Oh really?" Lewis was surprised.

"Yes," Johnson continued, "he had information on the nightclub drive-by."

"Interesting." Lewis stroked his chin. "Think it's connected?"

"No doubt," Johnson returned. "The killers must have doubled back and saw us."

"What kind of leads do you have?"

"The vehicle in the drive-by was a beat-up older-model Chevy, four-door, black. There were two suspects, driver and gunman. It appeared the shooting was a random act of violence, but now with Reese's death I think it was intentional. They just didn't kill the right person."

"So you think the girl was in the wrong place at the wrong time."

"Absolutely!" Johnson was sure of it.

"Sounds logical to me — what about you, Manny?"

"I agree with my partner, Edgar, because I think someone from the club knew something but just didn't tell it."

"Well, with no witness we're back at square one," Lewis stated as they nodded in agreement. "Anyway, you two go over to the Reese place and check it out."

"On our way," said Johnson.

"One more thing, did you record the conversation?" he asked.

"No sir, I just jotted down a few notes," Hernandez answered.

"Ground zero!" Lewis spoke the truth as he resumed unpacking.

Johnson and Hernandez turned around and headed for their service vehicle. Taking the ten-minute drive to Reese's home, they found the setting rather quiet for a murder scene. There was the normal assortment of evidence techs, coroner's van with staff patiently waiting, beat cops, and family members, plus curious onlookers, but missing was the horde of media personnel that usually gathered at crime scenes in hopes of providing the day's top story.

Johnson parked, then he and Hernandez got out, relieved that they weren't immediately bombarded with questions from the handful of beat reporters on the scene.

"Are you Sergeant Johnson?" a young lady asked while stepping forward.

"Yes, I am, and you are...?"

"Beverly Reese." You could tell she'd been crying.

"Ms. Reese, I'm sorry about your loss. Let me check out the scene then I'll get back to you." Johnson started to go inside but she blocked his path. "You'd like to talk first?" he said sincerely.

"Hell yeah, I'd like to talk first!" she screamed.

"Calm down, ma'am, step over here." He motioned to an unoccupied area of the street.

"I ain't steppin nowhere!" She was angry. "What I want to know is why my daddy had your business card in his hand when I found him dead!" she hollered, displaying Johnson's blood-stained card for all to see.

"That's evidence — you should not have tampered with it," he said.

"Man, that's my goddamn daddy up there and I want answers!" she spewed.

"Come with me," Johnson demanded while lightly tugging her arm.

With this bit of "news" the reporters were on their cell phones, and before Beverly's words had time to sink in, they had a blockbuster. Beverly, Nate and Manny walked past the officers posted at the door, then stopped to survey the broken glass on the floor. The killer had knocked out a single windowpane on the door to gain entrance by reaching through and letting himself in the building.

"Nothing on the glass or the door, Sarge," said the tech who had completed the ritual of dusting for prints.

"Thank you, Tracy," Johnson said.

"You still haven't explained why my daddy had your card," Beverly growled through clenched teeth.

"Ms. Reese, let me finish the investigation, then I'll answer all your questions, OK?"

"Hell naw, you gonna answer me now. I have a right to know!" she shouted.

"I understand that, Ms. Reese, but I'm not at liberty to disclose information to you."

"Oh, so you ain't gone tell me nothin!" She was indignant.

"Let's go upstairs," he said.

"I ain't goin back up there!" She meant it.

"Souza." Johnson motioned to a uniformed officer. "Take Ms. Reese out to your patrol car and keep her there until I come out," he barked.

"Yes sir," the officer obeyed.

Johnson and Hernandez barged up the steps to survey

the murder scene while Souza and Beverly went outside. Reese's lifeless figure lay on the floor covered with his own sticky blood. Hernandez, who had remained silent throughout the entire ordeal with Beverly, finally spoke.

"It don't look good, Nate," he said.

"What's that, partner?" Johnson asked, not really hearing the words because his mind was pre-occupied with the Beverly tirade.

"None of this." Hernandez was emphatic. "I mean, we interview the witness, the witness comes up dead holding YOUR business card, his daughter finds it. . . . It don't look good, Nate. She's probably holding court with the press right now!"

Johnson walked over to the window that Reese loved to sit at and peered onto the street below. Just as his partner had assumed, Beverly Reese was holding court with a throng of reporters, their cameras shoved into her face. He wondered how in the world those television crews could get there that rapidly, but knowing bad news always travels swiftly, he understood that the media wanted the sensational headline-grabbing stuff to boost ratings.

"OK Manny, let's go face the music. Wrap it up, guys," he hollered to everyone. "This one's gonna be tough."

They slowly marched down the steps and outside, only to be greeted by flashbulbs blinding them and microphones shoved in their faces. Beverly Reese stood with arms folded, glaring menacingly at the two detectives.

"Sarge, is this murder related to the killing last night?" asked one reporter.

"Why did the victim have your business card in his hand?" shouted another.

"Was he a witness?"

"Did he die because of what he saw?"

"What about his favorite chair?"

"What did he tell you?"

The questions came rapid-fire, and the entire scene would be broadcast on every local newscast that evening. Johnson stepped up to the microphones and waited until everyone became silent.

"Ladies and gentlemen, once our investigation is complete, we will disclose full details of the case. Then and only then will I be able to answer your questions."

Giving Hernandez the eye, Johnson led as they bulled through the crowd, got into their car, and drove off. As they pulled away a bottle clanked against the windshield, along with several rocks. Uniformed officers broke up the potential mob scene as Johnson wheeled his way back to headquarters. They entered the building through the side door on Washington Avenue, only to be met by Lewis, who was calm.

"Nathan, it doesn't look good."

"Don't I know it," Nate sighed.

"The story is on every television and radio station, and most likely will be in every paper tomorrow. The good point is you followed departmental rules to the letter and didn't divulge pertinent information. You guys take the rest of the night off and I'll see you tomorrow."

"Thanks, man," Johnson said as he and Manny walked away.

Johnson was a pro's pro and knew that even though the public's court of opinion was currently giving the police a black eye, all he had to do was solve the killings and everything would be alright. He was happy that Edgar Lewis had been promoted to head of the homicide unit, because their old boss Spitz probably would have had a stroke from the day's drama. Lewis was calm throughout the entire ordeal.

Lewis knew Johnson would be no good tonight because his mind would be pre-occupied by the press conference and Beverly. Johnson was happy that his new supervisor understood. He and Manny walked to the employee parking lot without speaking, each man absorbed in his own thoughts.

"See you tomorrow, Manny."

"OK Nate, have a good night's rest, amigo."

Johnson got in his Benz, Hernandez his Lexus, then they both headed in opposite directions — Nate to Antioch, Manny to Castro Valley. Nathan was sure Manny would fill his wife in on the details of the day's activities, but Nathan would also tell his own wife his version. Tomorrow, they would report for duty and try to find a fresh lead.

12
NUMBER ONE

Silky walked out to the parking lot and de-activated his alarm, which also unlocked the doors. As he was about to slide into the Mongoose, he peeped a note on his windshield held in place by the wiper blade. Lifting it off the window, he closed the door, turned on the overhead light, and read it.

Hi lover,

All I can think about is you, you felt so good inside of me. I will be up very late tonight so if you get this note, walk through the courtyard slowly and when I see you I'll meet you at our spot. I went back and left the window unlocked, along with locking the door for the manager, so no one will know we are there. If you can't make it, call me tomorrow and let me know when we can be together.

Your Secret Lover

Silky reread the letter several times and considered taking that stroll through the courtyard, but it wasn't his style to stand a woman up after giving his word. Ripping the note into shreds, he started the engine, tossed the paper out the window, and drove away. Rolling up to the Eagle at one-thirty, he was surprised to see Melody and Marv standing outside waiting. Marv said goodnight to Melody and got in his car while she hopped into the Mongoose.

"Hi, baby," she said, kissing him on the lips.

"What's up?"

"You'll never guess what happened," she stated.

"The club closed early," he said matter-of-factly.

"Yes, but that's not what I mean."

"What happened?" he asked her.

"Take a guess, honey," she giggled.

"There was a bomb threat so fat Ollie closed early and let y'all go home."

"Silky, you so crazy," she laughed. "What happened is Ollie closed early because business was non-existent."

"That's it."

"No, that's not it."

"Well, what is it, baby?"

"Alright, I'll tell you. After we left last night, those two detectives went across the street and questioned this old dude named Uncle Bob. He came into the club from time to time to get his head bad — nice old man. Anyway, after they left his house, somebody killed him. Now here's the juicy part — his daughter Beverly went to his house and found him stabbed to death with the black dude Johnson's card in his hand. Marv said the block almost turned into a riot scene because people were mad, claiming Five-O caused Uncle Bob's death."

"That bad, huh?"

"Honey, that ain't the half of it," she continued. "TV cameras, reporters, everybody who was anybody was on the block. They must have just left before you got there. I heard that a whole lot of people got busted. Those fools were throwing rocks and bottles at police cars ... it was a madhouse."

"Damn!" Silky shouted, his mind on Skye.

He eased the Mongoose into her stall, grabbed his overnight bag to her delight, and they went up the stairs to her pad. Melody wore red short shorts plus matching high heels, along with a skimpy halter top. She looked good. Knowing that most men who visited the club wanted a piece of her but she only wanted him caused Silky's ego to go overboard.

"That's a cool-ass panther," he said as they entered the apartment.

"It's not a panther, baby, it's a Manx — you see the tail clipped off?"

"Oh yeah, I see what you're saying," he replied, embarrassed.

"It's alright, honey, most people don't know it," she said.

Melody began undressing right in front of him, then took his hand and led him to the bedroom. Silky stripped down and joined her in bed with a million thoughts running through his brain. Why did Skye want him dead? How would he get that fool? Who did he want more,

Melody or Bridgette? What did the old man know? Who killed him?

Before his brain had time to answer, Melody was sucking his dick like a frozen popsicle on a hot summer day. Silky closed his eyes, enjoying the sensations. When he finally came, she gulped it down like a soda, vocal cords squealing with delight. He was exhausted and hadn't done a thing. She smacked her lips as if she'd just eaten a five-course meal, then placed her head on his chest.

"Honey, I know you got a lot of women, so I'm probably number fourteen, but do you think I'm asking too much of you to say don't get number fifteen, then let number fourteen rise up to number one on the charts?"

"I ain't got no fourteen, and as far as I'm concerned, you are number one," he said drowsily.

"Good! Because I know with some hoes it takes time to get rid of 'em, but I want to be your main squeeze. I love you and I think you already know that — what worries me is that you have so many women. Now, I'm prepared to deal with that shit if I know I'm the one you truly want. Let me be direct: As far as I'm concerned, you're now officially my man and I intend to keep you, so those hoes better understand that they have serious competition. Is that agreeable to you?"

Melody looked up in the darkened room at Silky, only to find him sleeping like a baby. She rolled over on her side and fell asleep too. Silky woke at noon the next day to a sweet aroma coming from the kitchen. Heading straight for the bathroom, he saw Melody in the kitchen cooking breakfast with nothing on except her high-heeled shoes. His manhood stiffened, causing him to have to pee by pushing his dick down at the toilet and holding it in place.

He went back to bed still hard, flicked on the noon news, and waited for his meal. The near-riot Melody had told him about was being shown so he turned up the volume. As the anchorman gave vivid descriptions of the grisly murders, Melody walked in holding his plate. She had prepared bacon, sausage patties, hash browns, buttermilk biscuits, scrambled cheese eggs, and fresh-squeezed orange juice.

"Breakfast is served, but my meal is staring at me," she said as she eyed his hardened penis.

"Thank you, babes," was all he could muster.

He began gobbling down his food like a man starved, which he was, while she watched in admiration. Once he was finished, she mounted him and got her groove on. Melody rose up and down on his meat as he watched his pole become lathered with her cream. Silky rolled her over into the missionary position and banged away with her screaming at the top of her lungs. Blasting off a powerful load of cream, he slid off and took a nap.

She woke up before he did, scooped up the tray, and went to clean up the kitchen. Since Monday and Tuesday were her off nights, Melody asked Silky if he wanted to do anything special.

"What time is it?" he asked, wiping matter out of his eyes.

"Five o'clock, honey — why?"

"No particular reason, I just wanted to know."

"You like movies?" she asked.

"Yes I do, but what I really need to do is handle my business."

"Would you like company?" she purred.

"I'd love it."

"Well, I'll be ready before you."

She walked out of the room, and the next thing Silky heard was the shower running. By the time he got up, she was toweling herself dry. He took a shower then went to get his overnight bag, surprised to find Melody fully dressed and patiently waiting for him on the sofa. She wore a body-hugging gold cotton dress cut low, displaying mouth-watering cleavage and barely covering her behind. With matching shoes, earrings, and handbag, she looked like a model.

"Let's go," he told her.

Silky was decked out in black Levis, silk shirt, and alligator boots. Like Melody, he was saturated in gold. He started up the Mongoose, easing his ride from the stall in reverse. After backing up, he shifted gears and cruised off slowly. Taking the streets, they stopped at several locations. At most of them he met a woman.

At each spot, Silky would go to the rear of the vehicle, lift out a package from his duffel bag, and go in. When he came out, some scantily dressed woman would give him a hug and kiss then go back inside. Every last one of them aimed for the lips, but Silky turned at the just the right time, giving them cheek instead. Melody sat in the Mongoose looking like a beauty queen, wondering how many of these skags Silky had blessed with his body, and if she wasn't there, how many would he kiss on the lips.

She now realized why his business was prosperous: women did his dirty work. Unlike men, they didn't stand on corners, had steady customers, and were discreet with their operation. The handful of dudes' homes he did stop at were all well-dressed and handsome, so Melody surmised that they were gay. Silky was international, dropping off packages throughout the city.

Melody admired his style but not what she saw, because his pit stops included Jingletown (Mexican), Chinatown, Rockridge (white), and Funktown (black), along with the lake (straight and gay) neighborhoods. When they pulled away from each location, he'd hand her a wad of cash and tell her to "hold this for me." The last stop was Tasha's pad. Silky rang the buzzer but she wasn't home.

"You hungry?" he asked Melody while sliding into the Mongoose.

"Kinda," she answered.

"Is fish alright?"

"Catfish?" she replied, hoping he would say yes.

"With oysters and prawns?" he answered her with another question.

"Yes, dear."

"Good, 'cause that's what I want too." He spoke the truth.

Silky went to Vida's for their meal, his favorite fish spot in the city. Their motto "U buy, we fry" is only the half of it. Located on the corner of 14th & East 18th, it is a small yellow-painted building run by a deeply religious family. The food is on hits, seasoned the way your mama did, and everyone is treated like family.

They went inside just before closing time and Silky ordered a catfish, oyster, prawn combination plate for Melody plus a buffalo fish dinner for himself. The smell of fresh fried seafood cooked in clean oil had their nasal passages wide open. He asked for macaroni salad instead of french fries with their meals.

"I've never been here, baby," Melody said.

"Gurlll . . . this is what fish is all about. Wait til you taste it."

Food in hand, they drove back to Melody's crib.

"I don't know why Tasha wasn't home," he told his woman. "Maybe she's mad because I didn't bring her package two days ago like I promised."

"Maybe she stepped out for a minute," Melody reasoned.

"Maybe so," he concurred, "but Tasha is my number-one moneymaker."

"Really?" Melody was surprised.

"Hell yeah, gurl, shidd, Tasha got all the lesbos hooked up."

"She's GAY?" Melody had surprise number two.

"They tell me Tasha will eat yo pussy better than I fuck it."

"Damn, I never would have suspected that shit!" Melody was dumbfounded.

"Why not?" he asked.

"Because she doesn't look it."

"Melody, is there a certain way lesbians are supposed to look?" Silky wasn't prejudiced.

"No honey, but you'd just think they'd have butch hair-cuts and act like men," she said.

"Baby," he responded, "some of the finest women I know are gay. You cain't be treatin 'em wrong 'cause of that. If yo ass was gay, I'd treat you the same way I do now, the only thing different about you would be your sexual preference. See . . . that's what fucks people up and where they need to change their way of thinking. Just because you like the same sex physically don't make you no less than another human being."

"I guess I never thought about it that way," she said solemnly.

"No, you didn't 'cause you doin like everybody else — stereotyping. See baby, gay folks get just as high as straight folks. Ain't a damn thang different about them from us except they like to make love to their same sex. Now all those Bible-totin muthafuckas gone hollah that it ain't right, but most of the Bible-toters I know raise holy hell from Monday til Saturday, then go to church on Sunday playin saint, but be in yo club gettin drunk as a skunk on Sunday night."

"You right about that!" she said, loving the fact he could get his point across that way.

Silky hit Greenridge Drive when his pager vibrated on his belt clip. He shifted the gear into park, turned the motor off, then looked at the beeper while Melody got out. The page was from Tasha; it had her cell phone digits on it, along with 911 emergency. He pulled his phone from the console/armrest, spoke in hushed tones while Melody waited outside the Mongoose, then told her, "Baby, I gotta go — business."

Before she had time to respond, he peeled rubber in reverse and hit scratch, zooming away. Melody stood holding the food, wondering what made him change all of a sudden. She hoped it was the phone call, not her conversation about gays and lesbians. Trudging up the stairwell, she went inside and nibbled at her food. All of a sudden, she wasn't hungry anymore.

13
GOT YO ASS

"Hello?" Skye spoke into the receiver.

"Hi." The voice was soft. "Remember me?" said Tee.

"How could I forget?" he answered.

"I'm glad you didn't," she said.

"Whatup gurlll...?"

"Wanna go out tonight?"

"You don't waste no time, do you?"

"Not when I know what I want."

"Where you wanna go?" he asked.

"I'd like to surprise you," she answered.

"How we gone hook up?"

"Meet me at the Screamin Eagle?"

"OK," he said, "what time?"

"In thirty minutes?"

"Dat'll work."

"Be there, baby," she said.

"I will," he responded.

Skye hung up the phone and proceeded to get dressed in his fanciest outfit, which was a black two-piece leather getup with a tight-fitting turtleneck sweater. He looked at Lou with a grin on his face, then told his road dog, "Ah'll see you in da moanin."

"Oh, you fitna make a booty call, huh?" Lou said.

"You know it, dog. Met this thick-ass bitch named Tee. The girl's legs look like tree trunks, so I know the pussy's tight. I'mo pop that muthafucka, though," he boasted.

"It's like that?" Lou grinned.

"Hell yeah, I'll see yo ass tomorrow. Handle mah business."

"You know it."

Skye stepped out, got in his ride, and drove to the club. Tee's car was already there, so he parked behind her and went inside. She sat at the bar sipping on a drink.

"Oh, you made it," she said while standing up then hugging him.

"Told you I would. Girl, you look good," he said while leaning back to admire her physique.

She wore a black silk dress with a split on the right side just above mid thigh. Skye let his eyes zoom in on the thick leg bulging out of the split when she kissed him. Caught totally off guard, his manhood stiffened as his brain went blank.

"Let's get out of here," she said.

"OK," he answered huskily.

The few customers in the club were watching Monday Night Football on the big screen, but their attention wasn't on the game. Skye noticed all the envious faces sneaking peeks at Tee's large behind switching out the door. He felt like a giant, strutting out as if he were the player of the year. Tee went to her car and unlocked the door.

"You ride with me and we'll come back for your car in the morning," she said, emphasizing the point that they would definitely spend the night together.

Skye had no objections and obediently hopped in the passenger side. He knew she wanted his ass tonight. Tee hiked up her dress to her hips, then slid in the driver's seat.

"I can't be ripping my clothes," she spoke out loud, more to herself than him.

"I ain't complaining."

She took Seminary up to the 580 freeway, rolled through the Maze, then headed north on I-80. Skye didn't care because he assumed they were going to some motel for sex. While she wheeled the vehicle through traffic, he stared at her meaty thighs. The Xscape jam "Understanding" was blaring from her sound system as Skye contemplated what he would do to her in bed. Tee took the Richmond turnoff, exited at 10th Street, rolled to Second & Cutting, then pulled into a dirt-covered parking lot.

"Where we at?" he asked.

"Le Cordon Blue," she answered.

"I heard about this place — don't they have strippers?"

"They sure do. Like your surprise?"

"Gurlll . . . I ain't fitna watch no niggahs strip!" He got nasty.

"Baby," she cooed, "the ladies strip tonight."

"Well, that's different," he said while getting out.

The club was located on the outskirts of the city near the San Rafael Bridge. Gray with blue trim, the exterior was plain-looking in appearance but big. About twenty cars were scattered in the huge parking lot, making Skye think the place was empty, considering the size of it.

They walked up to the entrance, with Tee paying the five-dollar cover charge for both of them. Once inside, it took a few seconds for Skye's eyes to adjust to the darkness. The DJ booth sat to the left, with restrooms next to it. An elevated VIP section was situated right behind that, along with table-and-chair seating for one hundred people. A large dance floor sat squarely in front of the seating area with the stage directly in front of that.

The Salt-N-Pepa jam "Shoop" blasted out of the sound system before Skye realized that a woman was onstage dancing. He and Tee claimed a table in the corner and watched the show. "Baby" was down to her red thong panties, gliding her legs up and down a pole. Her nipples were fully erect and Skye was in a trance gawking at the fine body in front of him.

He peered around the room and saw nothing but men, many wandering to the stage to place bills into the homegirl's underwear. The only women in the joint were dancers, waitresses, and his date.

"She wont mah dick ta be hard tonight," he thought to himself.

The lady left the stage, then the emcee introduced the next dancer. "Keep Ya Head Up" by 2Pac blasted from the speakers as Pineapple strutted onto the platform. The place went wild. Pineapple was a nicely built Oriental/Black half-breed with legs you would die for. She wore a wrap-around Hawaiian skirt, psychedelic bra, and straw hat.

"What'll you guys be having?" the waitress asked.

"I'll have a virgin Margarita — what about you, babes?" Tee asked Skye.

"Uh . . . brandy and coke." His attention was on Pineapple pulling off her wraparound.

After the waitress left, Skye asked Tee, "Where da bathroom at?"

"It's next to the DJ," she answered.

Skye headed for the restroom with his eyes still onstage. Pineapple was now down to her thong, bent over wiggling her butt to roaring approval. He returned to the table and immediately gulped down his drink. Getting the waitress' attention, he was about to order another when Tee whispered in his ear.

"I want you now — let's go to my place."

"Awight, less go," he said.

They walked out holding hands before Skye put his arm around her waist, grinning at all the drooling men in the house. Stopping at the stage, he stuck a twenty in Pineapple's underwear, placed his hand on Tee's behind, and laughed out loud. She was the first woman he'd ever met who wasn't insecure. He knew they would be together for a long time.

The cool night air caused Tee's nipples to stand at attention. She unlocked his door, wrapped her arms around his shoulders, and kissed him savagely. They rolled away listening to "Can We Talk" by Tevin Campbell. Tee started talking about the special surprise she had in store for him as Skye listened silently. He was aware of his surroundings and what was going on, but his body and brain were at a standstill. By the time Tee rolled up to their destination,

Skye was like a zombie. She helped him inside then went into another room.

The house, located on Congress Avenue, belonged to her uncle, who had recently passed away. Tee would go by daily just to make it appear like someone was living there. Painted white with black trim, it was a small two-bedroom flat in need of a fresh coat and yard work. Since her uncle had no children of his own to inherit the home, her family squabbled about who would move there, as if the place were a mansion. Until they could come to an agreement, she volunteered to look after it.

Twenty minutes later, Silky and Junebug knocked on the front door, both giving Tasha a hug as they entered.

"Good shit, baby!" Silky congratulated her on her work. "How'd you get his ass?"

"I ain't tellin y'all my secrets 'cause if I did, you'd be trying to steal my game!" she laughed.

"Tasha?" Junebug asked.

"What baby?"

"How many times I got to tell you this? I could take any woman you got 'cause not only will I lick it — neutralizing yo shit — I'll also stick it, and believe me when I tell you, the broad gone choose me every time!" Junebug stuck his chin out proudly.

"Junebug, I've forgot more game than you'll ever know, fool!" she said cracking up.

Silky joined her in laughter while Junebug mumbled "Yeah, right" to both of them, looking Skye directly in the face.

"Girl, why his ass ain't tied up?" Junebug questioned.

"No need," Tasha said nonchalantly.

"Why not?"

"'Cause his ass ain't goin nowhere. Silky, I told you this clown ain't got no game — I'ont know why you even fool with his ass."

"What you give him, that sex drug Ecstasy?" Silky inquired while grinning broadly.

"Hell no, I gave his ass some GHB," Tasha bragged.

"GHB, I've heard of that. Doesn't it keep you awake and sort of knowing what's happening, but not really knowing?"

"Correct, dude, that's why he's sitting there looking stupid. He can see us and probably knows it's us, but cain't move a muscle and don't know what we talkin about."

"Damn!" Junebug shouted. "You gone have ta give me some of that shit to use on those stuck-up bitches I run into!"

"Told you da niggah ain't got no game," Tasha said to Silky.

"Ah don't give a damn what you say, gurl, ah wont some of that shit," Junebug repeated.

"What about you, Silky? You want some too?" she asked.

"Honey, I don't need no help in the romance department. I want the girl to know what's happening. Now Junebug been known to fuck a corpse, so him begging for a little help don't surprise me at all."

The three of them looked at each other, then they all burst out in laughter.

"I'ont care what y'all say — she ghin me some uh dat shit," Junebug stated.

Tasha reached into her purse and handed Junebug a vial

of the colorless, odorless potion of poison she had secretly poured into Skye's drink.

"Now 'Bug, you only need a few drops of this shit. What you do is put it into their drink, let it work, and by the time they wake up the next day naked in your bed, you should be licking it like you claim you can. If you're as good as you say." She glanced at Silky and grinned, "They won't care why they're letting you work them over and loving it, but knowin yo ass like I do, you'll probably be drunker than them and facing a date-rape beef."

"Fuck you, Tasha," Junebug said while curiously examining the liquid before continuing, "What we gone do wit da niggah?"

"Tasha, since you want him in the worst way, you call it," said Silky.

"OK, here's the plan. We tie his ass to that padded metal chair in the kitchen, then wait til he wakes up in the morning. Yaw can go home but be back by ten — the shit should be done woe off by den."

"Where's his car?" asked Silky.

"In front of Renee's chalk line — I call it an eye for an eye."

"We gotta move it," Silky said while lifting Skye's keys from his pocket.

"Why?" shouted Tasha.

"Baby, you don't know what he got in there. If the rollers tow it and the gun's there, that leads them right to you." He had a point.

"I see what you sayin," she agreed.

"'Bug and me will get the car and take it to Uncle James, and you know he'll strip it in a day!"

"Alright, that's the plan then," she said.

"See you in the morning, baby." Silky hugged her good-bye.

Silky and Junebug walked out, went to the club to get Skye's ride, then dropped it off at Silky's uncle's house. After that, they returned to get Junebug's Mustang.

"Where you headed, dude?" Junebug asked while getting out.

"I'm going to the crib, man. I need some sleep."

"Know that's right. I'm kinda tired myself."

"See you in the morning," Silky said.

"Later, bro."

Each man drove off in opposite directions.

14
A HELPING HAND

Johnson trudged through the office door early on Tuesday and went to his desk. He hadn't slept much the past two nights because his mind was preoccupied with his problems. Edgar Lewis walked in, casually sitting down next to his fellow officer, and started the conversation.

"Nate," he said, "I'll be straight — your card the daughter picked from Reese's fingertips is stirring up trouble."

"Don't I know it," Johnson deadpanned.

"This one's different. The media is blaming you for the guy's death, and the public is demanding an explanation as to what was spoken between the two of you."

"I can't divulge that information because it will ruin the investigation."

"Nate, you know I know that, but the problem is even when you do solve the case, you'll still be blamed for the guy's death."

Hernandez entered the office looking tired. He never handled pressure well, and even though it was Nate who was taking the heat, he knew sooner or later that some reporter would corner him for details of their conversation with Reese. The thought of that caused his stomach to churn.

"Hey guys," he said as he joined them.

"How are you doing, Manny?" Lewis asked as Nate shook his partner's hand.

"I'll make it," he said. "What's happening?"

"I was just about to tell Nate that Reese's daughter Beverly has hired our old friend Ralph Givens to represent her family in a wrongful death lawsuit."

"Damn!" Hernandez screamed. "I should have known that asshole would come crawling out from underneath his rock."

"Calm down, dude," Lewis said before continuing, "he's just doing his job like we do ours."

Ralph Givens was a policeman's worst nightmare because anything remotely resembling wrongdoing would result in him filing a lawsuit, which he usually won. Little to their knowledge, he was downstairs holding a press conference at that very moment.

Johnson sat resting his face on his massive palms, his mind a million miles away. He'd replayed the meeting with Reese over in his head hundreds of times, yet it still didn't make sense. The man had only given him a vague description of the getaway car and noted that two people were in it. He couldn't figure out why someone killed the guy over that — it just didn't add up.

"Nate . . . Nathan!" Lewis yelled.

"Oh yeah, what?" Johnson said, returning to Earth.

"Like I was telling Manny, you two solve this murder and do it fast, because I can only hold off the press for so long, OK?"

"We're working on it now," responded Johnson. "Let's go, Manny."

"Where you headed?" asked Lewis.

"To visit an old friend," Johnson said as they walked out the door.

The two detectives left without another word spoken. Heading for the transportation lot, they gassed up their service vehicle then sped off. Nate wheeled the blue Crown Victoria onto the 980 freeway, then headed east on 580.

"Where we going, man?" asked his partner.

"To get information."

Exiting at High Street, Johnson hooked a right on Agua Vista and eased up to the curb. The young man watering his lawn smiled when he saw them. Hernandez grinned upon seeing the dude. He was a young black guy with a large medical bandage taped onto the left side of his face.

"Johnson and Hernandez, my two favorite cops," he said, releasing the nozzle.

"Rainbow, how are you?" said Johnson, giving him a bear hug.

"I was fine until you broke my ribs," he said laughingly.

"Rainbow, how do you feel, man?" asked Hernandez, shaking his hand.

"Pretty good, pretty good. Hey, I heard you guys came to the hospital to visit me, thanks man," he said to both of them.

"We were concerned." Johnson spoke the truth.

"Man, that's nice to know, but knowing you two like I do, trouble must be close behind. I saw the news, Nate, and it looks like you're in trouble."

"I wouldn't necessarily call it that, Rainbow, but I do need your help," said Johsnon.

"My help — what kind of help?"

"I need you to find out anything you can about the murders committed Saturday night."

"What makes you think I can help you?"

"Not much except the fact that you beat us to every clue with your brother's killing. What I need is someone from the streets investigating for me because I'm a marked man. No one will talk to me now if their life depended on it. Matter of fact, they'll probably think their life does depend on it. I'm hot."

"Don't you guys have informants?" Rainbow asked while playing with his dog.

"They're not even helping on this one," Johnson said.

Rainbow looked at the two detectives and saw the desperation on their faces. Not knowing how he could be of assistance, he nonetheless couldn't turn his back on them. Besides, he surmised, they were there for him when he was caught in the crossfire of the drug wars.

"Go to the back, Iceberg," he told his pure-breed German shepherd.

"Woof!" barked 'Berg, happily running up the driveway.

"Now, what do you want me to do?" Rainbow asked Johnson.

"Just see if you can find out about the shooting at the nightclub, because whoever did that probably bumped off the old man. Now if you feel it's too hot to handle, back off. By the way, I see your stuttering is gone."

"Yes it is — the doctors say in about nine months my handsome features will look almost good as new." They all grinned.

"Here's my card — I've written my cell phone number on it. Good luck and be careful."

They shook hands before Johnson and Hernandez drove off. Rainbow wrapped up his water hose then went into the house. Changing clothes, he dressed in blue Levis, brand-new black sneakers, white T-shirt, black Raiders golf cap, and a blue and white checkerboard shirt coat. Locking the front door along with closing the curtains, he went out back, filled Iceberg's water bowl and food tray, then hopped in Bertha, which is the name he'd given his money-green Honda Accord. Rainbow pulled slowly down his driveway in reverse.

"You think he can help?" Hernandez asked his partner.

"If he can't, nobody can. Rainbow has his own way of doing things, but it works because the dude knows every riff-raff in town, and as you know, people talk."

"Just not to us!" Hernandez stated truthfully. "Where we headed now?"

"Let's go find people on our witness list, starting with that girl Tasha," said Johnson.

"Sounds good to me."

They went to Tasha's crib but she wasn't home. Going down their list, every stop they made produced nothing. It appeared to them that the past two hours were wasted. Frustrated, Johnson headed back to the station when his cell phone rang.

"Johnson here!" he boomed through the mouthpiece.

"Check on this dude named Louis Arterberry, street tag is Toothless. He hangs out at a drug house on 65th & Outlook. Also look for his partner Skye Barnes. He's the violent one," said Rainbow.

"Thanks for the info, man. I owe you one." Johnson was sincere.

"Oh yeah, Toothless drives a beat-up black Chevy."

"That sounds like our guy," said Johnson.

"Be safe, bro." Rainbow hung up.

Johnson accelerated to headquarters, filling in Hernandez as he drove. His partner concurred that Arterberry's car fit the description.

"I still can't figure out how that guy finds out shit easier than we do," Hernandez said while scratching his head.

"He's from the streets, Manny, knows exactly where to go for information, and probably pays them with drugs or booze to get it. I have to admit he'd make a damn good detective. When this is over we'll ask him to join the force."

"What if he says no?" asked Hernandez.

"We'll make him give us his trade secrets!" Johnson laughed heartily. He felt good.

Johnson parked right in front of the building in a stall designated "for police vehicles only," then they got out, marching directly to their boss' office.

"Edgar, we have suspects," Johnson hollered loudly.

"Good, let's go pick them up," said Lewis.

"It's not that simple," said Johnson as his chief sat back down.

"Why not?" he inquired.

"The suspects hang out at a drug house on 65th & Outlook, one Louis Arterberry a.k.a. Toothless, and Skye Barnes."

Lewis understood. Five-O couldn't just send an officer to a drug spot without serious backup. The possibility of gunplay always loomed large.

"So what we'll need is a search warrant, the narc squad, and the tactical unit," Lewis said while stroking his chin.

"Exactly," Johnson agreed.

"OK, you guys go upstairs and see if we have the suspect's mug shot on file. I'll get the warrant and a team of officers. Meet me here in fifteen minutes."

"On our way, boss," Johnson said.

Johnson and Hernandez took the stairs to the third-floor identification office, where they poured through a stack of photos in the "A - C" file cabinet. The filing of photos was done by first initials of the last name, but since officers routinely sifted over them, not putting them back in order, they had to browse for the names and faces they were seeking.

Locating Arterberry's and Barnes' mug shots, they stuffed

the remaining photos back into the drawer, ran off thirty color copies, and made a beeline back to their office. Lewis was already there, along with a crew of twenty officers discussing the game plan they would use. Johnson handed each officer a photo of Toothless and Skye as his boss spoke.

"Ladies and gentlemen, we need these two alive, so shoot only if your life depends on it."

"What strategy are we going to use?" Johnson asked Lewis.

"I forgot you two weren't here yet. We'll surround the area, cordon off the block, then ask the occupants out with the bullhorn."

"What if they don't comply?" someone asked.

"Then we have a standoff," Lewis answered. "Thad is here for that purpose." He pointed as Thaddeus Stevens tipped his hat in acknowledgement. "OK, guys, let's roll."

Five-O rolled up to Da Spot, re-directed traffic, cordoned off the area, and alerted residents to vacate their premises, creating a ghost town. Lewis grabbed a bullhorn from his cruiser and spoke.

"THIS IS THE POLICE. THE PLACE IS SURROUNDED. COME OUT WITH YOUR HANDS UP!!"

One by one people exited the unit with their arms raised high in the air, but neither Toothless nor Skye were among them. Johnson and Hernandez questioned the prisoners as they were handcuffed and placed into individual patrol cars, then informed their supervisor that only Toothless remained. Barnes hadn't been seen for at least twenty-four hours. Lewis motioned for Detective Stevens, who pranced over like a superstar with mobile phone in hand.

Thaddeus Stevens resembled a nerd standing five feet nine, one hundred and thirty pounds. He wore bifocals, an outdated gray suit, run-over black shoes, and his trademark gray brim with black band and yellow feather. Square as he appeared, he was the best negotiator the department had to offer. Dialing the number given him, he went to work when Toothless answered on the third ring.

"Mr. Arterberry?" Stevens spoke softly.

"Yeah, what da fuck yaw wont?" screamed Toothless.

"We just want to talk to you, sir."

"Ah ain't got shit ta say!" he yelled.

"Sir. . . ."

"Look, you muthafuckin cop, ah said we ain't got shit ta talk about."

"I think we have many things to discuss." Stevens remained calm.

"Man, fuck you." Toothless slammed the phone down roughly.

He knew they must have figured out he was part of the drive-by, but without Skye there for leadership, Toothless was lost. Peeping out the window he saw marksmen on rooftops, uniformed officers hiding in every crack of the parking lot, and the Five-O helicopter hovering above, illuminating the front of the apartment with light.

The phone rang again, with Toothless picking it up then slamming it back down. Stevens was relentless in his approach so he kept calling at ten-minute intervals, with no success. The media arrived, only to create a circus atmosphere. Spotting Johnson, they assumed that this situation must be related to his predicament.

Johnson saw all the reporters pull up and told his boss that it would be best if he and Manny waited at headquarters. Lewis agreed, so they got in their service vehicle and drove off. They decided to spend the night at the station so that when Toothless was captured, they would be there to question him first.

The standoff lasted well past midnight. Johnson decided to take a catnap in one of the interrogation rooms, while Hernandez continued to sit by the phone. Around four in the morning, the phone rang. Hernandez groggily answered then snapped to immediate attention. Stevens had talked Toothless out safely, and they were bringing him in.

"Nate!" Manny shook him. "They got his ass — they're bringing him in."

Johnson rose up wiping his eyes. Lifting his spare suit off the rack, he headed for the basement showers for a much-needed bath. He knew that it would be at least two hours before Toothless was fingerprinted, strip-down searched, and processed. Manny grabbed his spare clothing and followed his partner. He felt dirty too.

They freshened up, went back upstairs to wait for their prisoner, then received a call about a dead body found in the industrial area. A man jogging with his dog stumbled across the corpse by accident because the dog wouldn't move from the spot. Since they were the only homicide detectives in the station, they had to go. They knew no one would question Toothless before Nate because his career was on the line.

Johnson eased his unmarked vehicle crookedly into a stall at the probation department. He and Manny talked briefly with uniformed officers standing guard before brushing aside the leaves covering the body.

"I'll be damned!" screamed Manny. "Shakey Jones!"

"Well, I'll be" was all Nate could say.

15
ALL YOURS

Silky guided the Mongoose into his stall at the Jamaican Arms, then activated his alarm while strolling casually to the crib.

"Hey." The voice he heard was familiar. "What are you up to?" Bridgette asked.

"Just going home to get some sleep," he answered truthfully.

"Long day?" she smiled.

"Very." He softened.

"Let me help you make it better," she said.

"How are you going to do that?"

"Like this." She showed him.

Bridgette wore a three-quarter-length leather jacket down to the knees, along with black high heels and a Dobbs brim. Opening the coat, she displayed her birthday suit. The girl was naked as the day she was born. Silky gawked at her fine frame and smiled, becoming instantly aroused by what he saw.

She looked delicious. Her ample bosom displayed no sag, jutting straight out like watermelons. Silky scanned the courtyard to see if anyone noticed them talking. Telling her to go to the back door, he went inside the front. Unlocking the sliding door, he let her ease past him. She tossed her coat onto the sofa.

He re-locked the sliding door and turned to face Bridgette. She stood like a trophy with her sculpted legs spread wide, high heels accenting every curve, and a mouth-watering stare fixated on the rapidly bulging lump in his trousers. She strutted over, looking him in the eye, then began kissing him with urgency while locking her legs around his waist. Silky broke the kiss, telling her, "Come to my bedroom."

Leading the way, he undressed as they marched up the steps of his townhouse unit. Silky turned around and kissed her sensuously while lifting the brim from her head, causing her hair to cascade down her back. She kicked off her heels as he slowly eased her down to the bed. His meat was throbbing on her belly as she tried to guide it in, but he was having none of that.

Silky kissed her softly on her mouth, cheeks, and neck, letting his tongue slide down to her tits. Licking around the areolas then flicking her pink nipples in a slapping motion with the tip of his tongue, he sucked and caressed her breasts for several minutes while she squirmed beneath him.

Making his way down to her navel, he left a trail of

saliva on her body, causing her legs to quiver. Nibbling around her stomach caused her to giggle, but he wouldn't stop. At the exact moment she attempted to pull his head up, he stuck his tongue into her prized possession.

Bridgette moaned loudly as Silky worked his magic on her hole. He toyed with her clit for a few minutes, but to her it seemed like hours. Love juice poured from her loins, soaking the bed, and when he placed the flat portion of his tongue over her vagina lapping up the cream, she screamed to the top of her lungs. No one had ever come close to making her feel this way. She was in love.

Letting off a powerful orgasm, Bridgette lay exhausted while her hole contracted. Silky raised his head to her face and kissed her passionately, allowing her a taste of her own cum. Forcing the tip of his large dick into her tight pussy, he fucked her with reckless abandon. Bridgette held on for dear life, moaning continuously as Silky rocked her world. She never knew sex could be this good. Blasting off his hot liquid into her, he lay motionless on top, letting her body absorb every drop.

Bridgette kissed his chest lovingly while their bodies remained entwined. Silky slid off, got out of the bed, and went to the bathroom where he took a shower. He returned to the room only to find her snoring loudly.

"Girl, you mine," he spoke out loud to himself.

Getting back under the covers, Silky eased up behind her into the spoon position with his arm wrapped around her, hand covering her breast. Three hours later Bridgette stretched her body and attempted to get up. Silky pulled her back down, rolled on top, and took her again. She had no objections, loving it all. Once he came, she spoke to her lover.

"I need to take a shower, and as much as I hate to, I have to leave. What time is it, anyway?" she asked.

"Three-thirty," he said glancing at the clock.

They both got up and showered together, washing each other's backs. Bridgette put on her shoes and brim then followed Silky downstairs, grabbing her coat off the sofa and putting it on.

"When will I see you again?" she asked.

"Whenever you like," he answered.

"I love you," she said while looking directly in his eyes.

"You barely know me."

"No, lover, I know all about you," she giggled while gazing at his stiffening penis. "I'd better go now or I never will." She meant it.

"Call me, baby," he said as he opened the sliding door.

"For sure," she said, kissing him lovingly then walking out.

Bridgette entered her home, put on a nightgown and hung up the outfit she wore, then went upstairs to join her husband Dino in bed. She couldn't sleep a wink because her mind was on Silky. She thought about the great lovemaking Silky provided, knowing her man could never satisfy her again. Making up her mind right there, Bridgette decided that she would quit him the next time they had an argument.

BEATEN TO THE PUNCH

Skye woke up with his mind in a fog. He couldn't remember anything from the night before. Groggily, he peeped out the room, not recognizing anything. The place was completely unfamiliar, and his head was pounding. Attempting to get up, he tumbled over, face slamming against the cold tiled kitchen floor. He was hog-tied to a metal chair.

"Surprise, motherfucker," said Tasha, kicking him viciously in the rib cage.

"Tee?" he shouted. "What you doin?"

"Mah-name-ain't-Tee-punk!" she slugged him after every word. "It's Tasha!" she screamed while stomping his face violently. "An dat was mah bitch you killed the other night. Yo ass gone pay."

Tasha was dressed in black jeans, tennis shoes, v-neck sweater, and her hands were gloved. Skye looked up with chills running through his veins. He knew he'd die today. He didn't understand why the woman he thought desired him one night earlier was now ready to chrome his dome. Tasha stood over his prone body ready for action, violent intentions on her mind.

Skye felt himself being lifted off the floor into an upright sitting position. Lip bloody, right eye swollen shut, and at the mercy of his captors, he scanned the room. The sight he saw caused his heart to do everything it could not to have an attack. His vocal cords went numb, because standing in front of him were Silky and Junebug. Their facial expressions displayed nothing but outrage.

Realizing they knew he'd done the shooting, Skye felt his throat swell up, making it impossible for him to speak.

"Skye Barnes," Silky asked casually, "why was yo ass shootin at me?"

"Silky, dat wadn't me, you know we tight man, ahm yo boy, dog."

Silky kicked him in the mouth with the metal-tapped heel of his alligator boot, causing Skye to fall over backwards. Junebug hoisted him up into a sitting position so they could resume their question-and-answer session.

"Who drove the car?" Silky asked.

"W-w-what c-c-car?" Skye stuttered.

Junebug hauled off with a solid right cross to his cheekbone, returning Skye to what was becoming a familiar place, the floor. He tumbled over sideways with his head banging against the tile again.

"Look punk, we ain't about no games. Tell us what we want to know and you just might live," Silky demanded.

"OK Silky, I'll t-t-tell y-y-you. I wasn't sh-shootin at you, I was s-s-shootin at dat niggah Byron 'cause he owes me m-m-money!" Skye cried out.

"Now I'll ask you again, who drove?" Silky said.

"It was m-ma-mah boy Lou, he drove. Man, p-p-p-please don't kill me!" he hollered.

Silky gave Tasha the "eye" as she stood in front of Skye with a large hunting knife. Junebug ripped a piece of duct tape from the roll and covered Skye's mouth. Tasha slowly carved the letters R-E-N-E-E into his skin deeply, happily watching the blood saturate his torso. His ovals grew larger than a dopefiend's on crack at midnight as he watched her plunge the knife deep into his heart.

The piece of tape covering his mouth pushed in and out as the muffled sounds from his vocal cords screamed in pain. Skye's head slumped over, dangling to the side as Tasha wiped her blade clean with a napkin. Licking her lips, she gazed at Silky with a look that caused him to think she enjoyed this madness.

"Let's go get Lou." She was serious.

The threesome placed Skye's lifeless body into an over-sized plastic bag, then as Silky and Junebug carried him out back, Tasha locked up the house. They drove off, tossing his body by the railroad tracks, then headed for Da Spot, where they knew Lou would be waiting.

Silky turned on Sixty-Fifth and saw police cars every-where, with traffic being re-directed and the street blocked off with yellow tape. Making a three-point turn, he parked up the block on MacArthur Boulevard. Getting out of the Mongoose while Tasha and Junebug peered from the open windows, he asked a spectator, "What happened, man?"

"Some fool up there with a gun," said the elderly gentleman.

"Wonder what causes people to do that?" Silky spoke.

"Don't know," said the guy "but dat place been a neighborhood dope house for years."

"Oh, dey at da dope spot?" Silky spoke ghetto slang.

"Yea, dat's where dey at," the dude said.

"Well, I hope no one gets killed," Silky returned and walked off.

Sliding into his hoopty, he told Tasha and Junebug what was going on, then they all began speculating.

"They probably raided Da Spot," said Tasha.

"I know they caught those sorry muthafuckas," said Junebug.

"Maybe they found out it was Skye and Lou who killed Renee," chimed Silky.

"Maybe so," said Tasha, thinking about her woman.

"Well," Silky concluded, "we can't get his ass today, I know that."

Tasha and Junebug agreed as Silky slowly maneuvered the Mongoose through the crowd. They would get the details by watching the evening news.

STREET GAME

Arroyo Park is located in the deep east side and covers eight city blocks. To a stranger it mirrors suburbia: two baseball fields, several hoop courts, dual parking lots on each end, a giant recreation center along with childcare facilities, and lush greenery providing a serene setting. There is a creek running through the park, tall eucalyptus trees everywhere, and convenient toilets for public use, along with a sandbox for kids.

Today the park was jam-packed as usual with joggers, basketball games, center activities for children, and drug dealers selling their poison. Rainbow killed the engine, got out of Bertha, and joined the madness in the undesirable back parking lot on the corner of Ritchie & Olive. He had a fifth of gin in his hand with the cap poking out of the bag.

Everybody knew him and noticed the large bandage on his face. They also knew how it got there. What they didn't know was whether he came to buy drugs or get even, so most of them steered clear. It was not uncommon in the ghetto for a victim of violence to be uncooperative with Five-O, then play vigilante themselves. You would have fifty eyewitnesses, but once the Man arrived, nobody saw a thing.

Ghetto residents have to live amid the madness on a daily basis and feel like the police don't care about their safety after arresting someone. Everyone knew the gung-ho officers would blurt out names in a minute, saying shit like "Joe Blow told me you pulled the trigger," hoping they would in turn rat on Joe Blow.

The minute the criminal was released or sentenced, all inside the pen or on the streets would label him a snitch. Overnight, he would become a walking dead man, so nobody wanted to be labeled. Rainbow spotted who he was looking for, bought a dime bag of weed, and sidled up to the man at the closed-down snack counter.

Larry Hawkins was the park freeloader, always searching for a free high. He also had diarrhea of the mouth — the dude couldn't hold a secret if his life depended on it. Always around but unnoticed, Larry heard everything because no one considered him a threat. Criminals talked freely of their crimes around this guy because all he was interested in was a drink or a joint, for free, of course.

He was a tiny man with an uncontrollable shake, until he got that first drink, then he was calm. "Lil' Larry," as he was called, stood five-three and weighed a feathery one twenty-five. Fifty years old, he had been an alcoholic for as long as anyone could remember. Lil' Larry was what could best be described as upper-class homeless.

Dressed in brown slacks with matching shirt and shoes, his appearance was passable, compliments of the free clothing he received weekly from the Mother Wright Foundation. He drove a beat-up '81 Olds four-door that served as a neighborhood taxicab. Anyone needing a ride to the store, methadone clinic, dope house, or just seeking to be dropped off somewhere could get it from Lil' Larry. Of course, it would cost them a bottle of liquor and a few bucks.

"Lil' Larry, wuz up?" Rainbow jived while noticing Larry had the shakes, flinching as if he were about to be hit.

"Ain't shit, 'Bow — heard you got shot, how you doin?" he said, greedily eyeing the liquor.

"I'm straight. Let me rap with you for a minute." Rainbow handed him the goodies.

Rainbow walked over to a bench near the hoop courts and sat down. Larry trailed behind, pocketing his weed and treating the booze like gold. He pulled the two cups from the bag and offered one to Rainbow.

"That's alright, man, I got that shit for you."

"Well, I guess I won't be needing these then."

Lil' Larry flicked the cups into the bushes behind him, then took a long swig from the bottle. After he swallowed, he let out a satisfied "ahhhhh," licked his lips, and took another drink before replacing the cap. The hoopsters began arguing loudly about a foul, which turned into a fistfight. Rainbow and Lil' Larry watched like everyone else, with amusement.

"What's goin on, homes?" Rainbow asked as the combatants were separated.

"Bullshit like that there," Larry said, hitting the juice again.

"I know, man, they be fightin for no reason, huh?"

"'Bow, niggahs will shoot you down for stupid shit. The world done gone mad."

"Dig it, I still don't know why I was sniped," Rainbow whispered staring at his rings.

"Man, ah heard bout dat, but ain't nobody talkin," Larry lied, holding a straight face.

"They tell me some fool did a drive-by at the Eagle the other night."

"Yeah, killed an innocent girl. If that was mah daughter, those niggahs would be six feet under."

Rainbow knew if that was Lil' Larry's daughter, he wouldn't bust a grape. He watched as the b-ball game resumed, paying no attention as Lil' Larry gulped down more gin.

"Know who did it, don't you?" Lil' Larry was ready to talk.

"Did what?" asked Rainbow, appearing unconcerned.

"The drive-by!" Larry squealed in his high-pitched voice.

"Don't know, don't care," Rainbow said, "I'm only interested in who shot me."

"'Bow, if I knew, I'd tell you, but I don't, man." He rolled up a joint.

Rainbow sat patiently as Lil' Larry took a drag then grunted as if he were trying to stifle a sneeze.

"Man, dis some good shit." He passed the joint to Rainbow.

"Dude, you know I don't smoke that shit. I just ain't seen you in a while and you know, when you're on your deathbed like I was, you start remembering all yo homies." What Rainbow said made Larry felt important.

"I know you tole me you don't care, but the dudes who did the drive-by was Skye an Toof-less. Niggahs was mad at Silky 'cause he takin over the business."

"Skye and Toothless, ain't they members of the empire?"

"No doubt, see, wit Big Ed in jail, Skye took over. The only person who had a problem wit it was Silky."

"Skye's last name is Barnes, right?" asked Rainbow.

"Yep!"

"Man, I never did know Toothless' real name, that niggah sorry anyway, ain't he?"

"Hella sorry!" Lil' Larry was on a roll. "His name is Louis Arterberry, and if it wasn't for Skye, his ass would've been kicked hundreds of times. All he do is drive while Skye do the gangsta shit. Skye done put him in charge of Da Spot on 65th & Outlook, but da niggah ain't nuttin moe than a figurehead."

Rainbow had the information he'd come for. Shooting the breeze with Lil' Larry a few more minutes, he rose to leave. They embraced then Rainbow walked to his ride while Lil' Larry joined the crowd in the parking lot. Everyone wanted to know what Rainbow wanted, so Lil' Larry held court.

"He wanted to know who shot his ass," Larry spoke

for all ears. "I told him, look dude, I'ont know and if ah did, you know ah cain't tell you that no way, 'cause my life is moe impotant than yose."

Satisfied with Lil' Larry's lies, the park dwellers resumed their normal activities, which was chaos at its best. Rainbow headed home, where he placed a call to Johnson to give him the names of the men they were after. Lying down, he took a nap.

COINCIDENCE OR CONNECTION?

Johnson and Hernandez waited by Shakey's dead body until their replacements arrived. When Derrick Boston and Maria Jimenez rode up, they immediately took over. They had been assigned the case by Lewis and were raring to go. Boston and Jimenez were Homicide's new kids on the block, appropriately labeled "hotshots" by staff detectives.

Both young and eager to make a name, these two were out to prove to all that they belonged on the team. Johnson considered them cool, not just because Maria was the first female assigned to Homicide, or Derrick had been the best undercover cop the vice squad had ever seen. He liked them due to their pleasant demeanor and personalities.

"Hey guys," Johnson greeted.

"Hello sir," they said in unison, causing Johnson to smile.

"What we have here is a violent felon named Shakey Jones — we know him all too well."

"The chief says he was found by a jogger," Derrick said.

"Correct, Derrick, but judging from appearances, he was killed yesterday."

"How do you know he was murdered, sir?" asked Maria.

"Throat slashed," returned Johnson, turning over the body.

"I see," said Maria. "Any witnesses?"

"None," said Johnson, "but I'm sure once staff arrives in that building" — he pointed at the probation office — "someone will tell you something."

"Thanks sarge," said Derrick. "Anything else we need to know?"

"That's it."

"Alright sarge, we'll take it from here," said Maria.

Johnson and Hernandez drove back to headquarters to question Toothless when another call blared across the radio transmitter. A dead body was found alongside the railroad tracks near 55th & San Leandro Boulevard. Manny informed dispatch that he and Nate were on their way. Pulling up to the scene, they walked past the assembled crowd and uncovered the sheet placed on the body by patrol officers.

"Damn!" shouted Hernandez. "Skye Barnes!"

"Partner, there are too many people we know coming up dead," said Johnson.

"You tellin me," returned Hernandez.

Since Skye was on their wanted list, they would investigate his murder, hoping to tie it in with the others. Johnson placed a call to a tired Deputy Chief Lewis, informing him of their intentions and reminding him to keep Toothless on ice. Lewis hung up the phone, left a memo on the door of the cell housing Toothless, then headed home. Hernandez had already begun examining the body.

"Nate, this killing has to be related to the nightclub shooting," he said with conviction.

"You're sure?" asked his partner.

"Positive — look at this." He pointed to the name "Renee" carved on Skye's chest.

"Manny, give me a toothpick," Nate said, noticing what appeared to be dirt under the fingernails.

Hernandez reached into his coat pocket and handed Johnson a toothpick; he carried them the way blacks carry hot sauce. Johnson used the toothpick to scoop out a portion of dirt from the nail then placed it in a zipock bag. He would have it examined and DNA-tested at the lab. Seeing the dark lines around Skye's wrists, he surmised that this man was tied up while the killing took place.

Johnson instructed the coroner's staff to take the body back to their laboratory and call him as soon as they knew the time of death, what the sticky substance was around his mouth, and anything else they could find. Hopping into the car with Hernandez following suit, the two detectives rolled downtown.

The station was overflowing with media personnel, prisoners, and transients. Johnson and Hernandez entered through the basement tunnel, then caught the elevator to the second floor. Strutting into Criminal Investigations

Division, or CID, they went directly to the interrogation room housing their witness. Hernandez marked the time before they entered. They would play the role of good cop/bad cop, with Johnson serving as the bad. Toothless sat handcuffed to a chair looking pitiful.

"Toothless, we got yo ass!" Johnson screamed while Manny looked on with sympathy.

"Got me for what?" asked Lou.

"Murder, motherfucker, that's what!" Johnson towered over him.

"Man, I ain't kilt nobody!" Toothless yelled.

"Look fool, Skye's dead." Johnson paused to let the point sink in before continuing. "You drove the getaway car in the drive-by, and whoever killed him wants you dead too."

"I'ont know what you talkin 'bout, man." Toothless' mind was on Skye.

Johnson flinched as if he were about to hit the suspect while Hernandez sprung into action, grabbing his arm. Toothless ducked for cover. Hernandez assumed his role of good cop.

"Louis."

"What, man?"

"We only want your cooperation. We know you were the driver and Skye did the shooting. What we don't know is why. Look, man, I'm on your side." Hernandez was convincing while Johnson continued to stare menacingly at Toothless.

"Man, ah tole yaw ah ain't drove nothin, man!" he cried.

"You a goddamn lie, muthafucka! If ah wadn't an officer of the law, I'd kick yo muthafuckin ass, punk!" Johnson balled up his fist as if to strike his prisoner.

"Toothless?" asked Hernandez.

"What."

"You want a cigarette?"

"No."

"Something to eat?"

"Ain't hungry."

"Do you want to make a phone call?" Manny seemed to be his friend.

"Maybe later I might want to call my mother," Toothless said.

Manny gave Nate the unspoken eye, which his partner had already picked up on. He left the room to go call Arterberry's mother, which was the prisoner's weak spot. Johnson placed the call and spoke to Toothless' mom, who'd been following the news reports with concern for her son's health. She hung up and came directly to the station.

"Mrs. Arterberry, how are you?" asked Johnson, showing concern.

"Ah jus wont mah son ta do the right thang, offisuh." She was toothless too.

"All we need is for you to convince your son to tell us what he knows, ma'am. Do you think you're up to it?" asked Johnson.

"Ah'll try," she said "Where he at?"

"I'll take you — follow me, ma'am."

Sharon Arterberry had followed Lou's criminal career

from juvenile halls to the youth authority and now as a mainline thug. She looked the part of poor mama trying to live respectably. Dressed in black polyester slacks, white ruffled blouse, U.C. Berkeley swim team jacket, and San Jose Sharks golf cap, she displayed welfare case for all to see. With a gang of family members tagging along professing Toothless' innocence, Sharon ignored them and followed Johnson to Homicide.

Toothless, who had been conversing quietly with Hernandez, sat straight up in his chair when his mother entered the room.

"Mama, get me outta here!" he screamed like the coward he truly was.

"Can ah have a few minutes wit mah son?" Sharon asked the detectives.

"Just knock on the door when you're ready to leave, ma'am," Johnson answered.

Toothless did a double take at Johnson's polite demeanor toward his mother. That asshole had done nothing but clown him; now he tried to play nice to the one person he loved.

"Mama, that dude is a fake," Toothless said.

"Shet up, boy, you lucky you ain't dead!" she chastised.

"Mama, I didn't do nothin," he whined.

"Louis, if you ain't did nothin, you wouldn't be here."

"Mama...."

"Mama mah ass!" she shouted "You tell dem what you know, den serb whatevah time dey gib you like a man, you understand?"

Toothless let out a sigh. "Mama, I ain't did nothin, you gotta believe me."

"Look boy, quit all dat lyin an tell dese folks what you know. You done already shamed yo family."

"But mama. . . ."

"Shet up, boyyyy, an do like ah tole you." She got up and starting bamming on the door.

Johnson opened the door, greeting her pleasantly, while Hernandez entered to resume his good cop/friend routine. Toothless' attention was on Johnson fooling his mom into thinking he was cool, and his anger returned.

"Man, dat muthafucka got mah mama thankin he all lat — that big black ugly niggah ain't shit!" he shouted.

"I know what you're saying, Toothless. I can call you Toothless, right?" asked Hernandez.

"Dass cool," he answered.

"You know, sometimes I don't like Johnson myself."

"You don't?"

"Hell no, man, he treats my people way worse than you, amigo. One day me and him gonna have it out 'cause of that shit."

"When yaw do, kick his ass foe me, man."

"I'll try, but as you can see, he's a big hombre," said Hernandez.

"Look Hernandez, ah got no beef wif you, man. I'mo be straight."

"Lay it on me, Louis," Hernandez said while pushing the record button on his tape.

"Dude, it went down like dis. Skye got mad at Silky 'cause Silky tried to take over the empire after Big Ed got busted."

"That would be Edward Tatum?" inquired Hernandez.

"Yeah, Big Ed," stated Toothless.

"Who is Silky?"

"Silky Johnson's dis punk-ass niggah who done got too big foe his britches. Skye was in charge now, but Silky didn't see it that way."

"What did Silky see?"

"Silky thought he was the better man, so he should be runnin thangs."

"And what was your role?" asked Hernandez, throwing Lou off track.

"I ain't had no role, man. Skye's mah road dog, so ah got ta show mah colors."

"So you drove the car at the drive-by shooting?" Hernandez pressed on.

"Yeah, I drove the car, but ah ain't shot nobody."

"Did you know the girl?"

"Naw, that was an accident. She was in the wrong place at the wrong time."

"So Silky was the target?"

"Yeah, only Skye missed."

"What I don't understand is why you guys killed the old man." Hernandez scratched his head.

"We didn't have nuttin to do wit dat."

"Toothless, be straight with me, OK?"

"I am straight, man, dat wasn't us."

"Excuse me for a moment while I go to the restroom."

Manny picked up his recorder and walked out. As soon as the door closed he clenched his fist and yanked it as if he had just scored the game-winning touchdown. Nate returned after walking Toothless' mom out and noticed the theatrics.

"Where's the dance routine?"

"What dance routine?" Hernandez asked.

"After a touchdown, they always do a dance!" They both laughed.

"Good news, Nate, listen to this." Hernandez rewound then played the tape.

Johnson listened intently while jotting down notes to himself. Once the tape ended he resumed his conversation.

"Manny, look at your witness list from the club and see if you have Silky Johnson's name on it."

"There's only one Johnson and his name is Duane," Hernandez said while gazing at his list.

"The guy who was with Tasha?"

"Si, amigo."

"Standing right next to Renee before she took the bullet. Manny, he knew they were after him. Tasha probably did too."

"Let's go pick 'em up," Hernandez stated.

"No partner, I think we should have them tailed for a day or two. I'm hoping they lead us to the murder scene."

"You think they killed Skye?"

"No doubt about it," said Nate convincingly.

"OK, we'll play it your way."

The detectives sat at their desks and began writing their reports. Once finished, they left them on Edgar Lewis' desk. Walking down the hall to the vice unit, they requested undercover surveillance on Duane "Silky" Johnson and Tasha Savoy. Since Toothless' taped confession of Renee's murder was signed, sealed, and delivered, all they had to do now was find Reese's and Skye's killers. Walking to the employee parking lot, Johnson spoke to his partner.

"Manny, I'm still puzzled by the old man's killing — it just doesn't add up."

"I know, Nate — the thing that gets me is what reason would someone have to kill the guy?"

"See you in a little while, man," said Johnson, getting into his ride.

They each drove home to get four hours' sleep, freshen up, then return for more drama.

SECRET WEAPON

Vanessa Harris sat in the living room of her modest two-bedroom home bored to death. A stranger in town, she felt all alone. The government had placed her in the witness protection program, creating a new identity, name, and background. The only stipulation was that she not contact any relatives or friends in Oaktown. They didn't want her homesickness to ruin the case they had built against Big Ed Tatum.

With the trial only one week away, Vanessa was antsy. She hated the name "Pamela Prescott" that was chosen for her, and her new city of Norwalk, Connecticut, was just too slow. She worried constantly about her parents, and being an only child, knew they had to be miserable without her.

Pacing the floor of her living room, she decided to call her mom. Picking up the phone, she dialed her parents' number.

"Hello," her mother answered.

"Mama, it's me," she whispered.

"Vanessa, honey, we're worried to death about you, baby." She motioned for her husband to pick up the other line.

"Mama, I'm fine, just bored."

"Where are you, baby?" asked her dad.

"Daddy, I miss you guys so much."

"We miss you too, pumpkin — now where are you?"

"Daddy, they got me in a city called Norwalk, Connecticut."

"When can we visit?" her father asked.

"Daddy, Momma, you can't. I'm not even supposed to call you, I just had to."

"Look, Ness," her mom said, "just do as they say and everything will be alright."

"OK mom, I have to go now but I just needed to hear your voices and tell you I'm fine. Don't worry about me, alright?"

"Alright baby, we love you!" said her mother.

"I love you more," she returned.

"Bye baby and take care of yourself."

"I will, mama. Bye, daddy."

"Bye baby," said her father.

Vanessa hung up the line feeling refreshed. It was good therapy for her to call her parents — she really missed them and Oaktown too, for that matter. She had to admit that she loved all the goodies the government lavished on her. A new home paid in full, new car, job, credit cards, and bank account, but the price was steep. What harm could one phone call do, she reasoned.

The dark blue van made a U-turn and rolled slowly down Malcolm Avenue in the Oaktown hills. Its two occupants' assignment was to tap the Harris phone line and eavesdrop until Vanessa called her parents. Knowing their mission was accomplished because they now had her location down to the street address in Connecticut, they placed a call to the number given them.

"Hello." Sweetpea spoke into the receiver.

"The person you want is in Norwalk, Connecticut," said the nameless voice on the other end.

"What's the address?"

Sweetpea lifted his pen off the coffee table and wrote down the address twice as it was called out. The phone line went dead as he tore the paper in half and placed one in his wallet and the other in his front pocket. Drooling at the photo of Vanessa, Sweetpea considered raping her first, then killing her because she was just that fine.

Realizing how important the job was and how much money he was being paid, he knew rape was out of the question. Calling the airport, he booked the next available flight. Sweetpea was an assassin for hire. His trademark was the switchblade and skills unmatched. The dude could flick a knife casually and hit a moving target ten feet away directly in the heart.

A distinguished-looking fellow, he stood six-one, had a salt-and-pepper afro, was lean in appearance, and aging gracefully at fifty. No one knew his real name or much about him, and he chose to keep it that way. The phone call he'd just received was to an untraceable cellular; his identity was unknown to all. Packing lightly a blue suitcase equipped with wheels, he locked the door of his

Fairmont Avenue penthouse, stepped up to the elevator, and turned the key, calling it to pick him up.

Driving his Mercedes 450 SEL to the Coliseum BART station, he parked and caught a cab to the airport. Giving the driver a twenty for the seven-dollar ride, Sweetpea lifted his luggage off the floorboard of the back seat and strolled into the airport. Paying cash along with displaying a phony driver's license for the name he'd used, he boarded the red-eye flight for his five-hour ride.

Once the plane landed at JFK Airport in New York, Sweetpea wheeled his luggage to a car rental counter and checked out a mid-sized sedan for his one-hour drive. Rolling onto the VanWyck Expressway, he crossed Whitestone Bridge, merged with I-95, and drove past the suburbs of Norwalk to the more urban city of Bridgeport.

Checking into a modest motel using his fake identification, Sweetpea took a shower, then steam-ironed the wrinkles from his beige slacks and shirt with the portable iron he'd brought. Next, he lifted the street map from his overnight bag, tracing the location he desired, then set out on his mission.

Heading first for the red-light district on Main Street, he entered a pawn shop and looked over the assorted knives for sale. Choosing two switchblades, he pressed the release buttons several times to see if they worked properly. Satisfied, Sweetpea paid cash and walked out of the store, small bag in hand.

Entering a packed greasy spoon, he ordered lunch. The daily special was meat loaf, mashed potatoes and gravy, spinach, rolls, and a soda. Sweetpea finished his meal, left a tip, and walked out. The meal was both tasty and served its purpose.

Getting into his rental, he got on I-95 for the twenty-minute ride to Norwalk. Exiting at The Post Road, which was the main thoroughfare, he parked four blocks away from Vanessa's crib.

No one paid attention to the well-dressed black man going into the young black woman's home. If they had, they still wouldn't have known he was picking the lock instead of using a key. Sweetpea was just that smooth. Pulling off his cream-colored gloves and stuffing them into his beige sport coat, he sat on the sofa and waited.

Meanwhile, at her job Vanessa sat at her desk amused by the office scene. The men were falling all over themselves for her attention, while the women displayed pure jealousy. She got up from her seat and walked to the water cooler for a much-needed drink.

"Hey Pamela?" her boss Joey called. She ignored him.

"Pamela?" he spoke louder.

"Oh ... oh ... what?" She'd once again forgotten her new name.

"We're going out for drinks after work and wanted to know if you'd like to join us."

"I don't think so, Joey. I make it a rule not to socialize with my co-workers."

Joey stood in front of her with his mouth hanging open as she sipped the water. He wanted to be first in the office to lay the fine filly standing in front of him. He had been sexually harassing her from the day she arrived, but Vanessa coyly ignored his advances. She would never sleep with a white man anyway, so his chances were null and void, only he didn't know it.

She continued sipping water as Joey drooled at her statuesque frame. Vanessa was a five-foot-eight, hundred-and-fifty-pound centerfold. Her measurements were 36-24-36, complexion high yellow, lips full and pouty, legs chiseled, and curves in all the right places. She was full of lumps, if you get my drift.

Tossing her cup into the trash can, she returned to her desk. As she did, the women in the office stared hatefully at her back. They were relieved by the fact that she turned Joey down, but wondered if she would do the same when their office lover made a play. Vanessa/Pamela watched the clock intently for the next twenty minutes then packed up her things and cut out.

Happy to be away from the drama, she stopped at a supermarket to purchase a bottle of white zinfandel. All movement seemed to stop as the fine black woman's butt switched with every step. The plain blue skirt she wore along with white blouse and blue jacket did little to cover her assets.

Sweetpea heard the automatic garage door open slowly and swung into action. Leaping up, he went to her bedroom and stood in a corner pulling out his blade. Vanessa placed her wine on the kitchen table then began undressing as she opened her bedroom door. She didn't remember closing it when she left that morning, but ignored the intuition.

As the door swung open, her eyes grew wide with fear. She attempted to scream but the lump in her throat wouldn't allow it. Even if it had, it would have been useless because the knife was already rotating towards her frame. The blade struck her directly in the heart and she crumpled to the floor like a sack of potatoes, shit pouring from her behind.

Sweetpea pulled the knife out of her body, then gazed lovingly at the half-naked woman lying dead before him.

"Damn, too bad I couldn't hit that!" he said to himself.

Wiping the knife clean of her blood, Sweetpea walked out of the front door and casually strolled to his rental. Driving back across the bridge, he returned the car, lifted his luggage from the trunk, then booked an on-call flight to Oaktown under his fake name. He left the city without a trace, dumping the knives in a garbage container at the airport. Pulling his untraceable cell phone from his sport coat, he dialed the number on a wrinkled piece of paper.

"Mission accomplished," he said then hung up.

Sweetpea took his seat on the plane and rode home content. Killing was the only avenue of entertainment he truly enjoyed. The fact that he could do it without leaving a trace satisfied this man tremendously. He'd be fine for a few months until the monkey on his back reared its ugly head once more, then he would kill again, for sport if necessary.

NIGGAH PLEASE

Silky sat at Melody's kitchen table shaking his head in disbelief at what she'd just said. It couldn't be true.

"Who else you been with?" he asked.

"Nobody Silky, except you!" Her eyeballs looked like two daggers.

"Then you must've had that shit before I met you and just found out about it today!" He was just as angry as she was.

"Look, Silky," she sat with her hands clasped, "I went for my pap smear, then they called me later and told me I had a disease, chlamydia to be specific. You need to check yo hoes." She got up and paced the floor before continuing her tirade. "I thought I was number one!"

"You are number one!" he spoke softly, staring at his hands.

"Obviously I'm not," she grunted.

"OK," he said, "what do you want me to do?"

"Get tested."

"Get tested for what? My piss ain't burnin."

"Silky, listen," her voice softened, "Chlamydia has no pee-burning symptoms, it's just there. Unless you're properly treated, it lingers." She handed him a pamphlet on the disease.

"Awight, let's go," he said.

They walked out, got in the Mongoose, and hit 580 for the ten-minute ride downtown. Each person was absorbed in their own thoughts, so the ride produced no conversation between them. Silky parked in a visitor's stall at the clinic, shutting off the engine. His piss wasn't burning, but he knew something was wrong because his penis had been leaking pus all day.

"You ready?" he asked.

"I ain't goin in!" she snarled.

"Then why'd you come?"

"Because I want to see the look on your face when you come out" was all she said.

The health clinic was located on 27th & Broadway and sat right behind Sizzler's Restaurant, directly across the street from a coin-operated car wash. Painted beige with brown trim, the building was small, housing only three floors. Silky stepped to the counter and spoke in hushed tones to the receptionist.

"May I help you?" she asked.

"Yes, I'd like to see a doctor."

"Nature of injury?"

"I want to get tested," he said quietly.

"What are your symptoms?"

"I just want to be checked."

"You think you've been infected?" she inquired.

"I don't really know."

"How will you pay?"

"Pay? I thought this was a free clinic!" His voice rose.

"Technically it is, but we ask those who are capable to leave a donation," she said, noticing how well-groomed he appeared.

"Is that enough?" he said as he handed her a twenty-dollar bill.

"That's fine," she responded. "Follow the yellow line on the floor to the waiting room, fill out this form, and the nurse will call you shortly."

Silky trailed the yellow line to the waiting room, instantly disgusted by the view. Its occupants resembled a homeless get-together. Derelicts, prostitutes, and dope fiends sat chatting away freely as if having a disease were natural. Sighing to himself, he chose a chair in the rear and began filling out his form. After a few minutes, his name was called.

"Duane Johnson," announced the nurse as he stood. "Follow me."

Silky followed her down the hall to the scales, where she checked his weight. Next, she instructed him to sit down in a chair provided, then took his blood pressure, pulse, and handed him a cup, telling him to go to the restroom and urinate. Returning with the cup full of gold-colored urine, Silky gave it to her.

"Have a seat," she ordered, and he obliged.

Setting up her blood-drawing unit, the nurse told him to make a fist. Locating a bulging vein, she wiped the area with an ammoniated gauze pad, then stuck the needle into his arm and watched as the tube filled with blood. Placing a cotton ball and tape on the hole left by the needle, she spoke.

"Apply pressure for five minutes, go back to the waiting room, and the doctor will see you shortly."

Silky went back to his chair in the waiting area, depressed by the sight. Having never been in a place like this before, he felt ashamed. The hookers in the room went out of their way to get his attention, incorrectly assuming that Silky was a pimp. They got up and strutted to the water faucets, restroom, or the front door just so he could view the merchandise. He ignored them all because his mind was on his own problems. When his name was called fifteen minutes later, the waiting area was nearly empty. The nurse led him down the hall into a room.

"Take off your clothes and put on this gown. The doctor will examine you in a minute," she said, handing him the blue paper gown and closing the door.

After hanging his clothes on the door hook, Silky put the gown on backwards, lay down on the examination table, and closed his eyes. There was a knock on the door but before he could speak, it was already being pushed open.

"Mr. Johnson?" the doctor asked while entering.

"Yes." He sat up.

"Hi, I'm Doctor Lowe and I'll be treating you today." She sat on a stool.

"Treating me for what?" he asked.

"Have you been having any problems urinating?" she proceeded, ignoring his question.

"No."

"Sex with more than one partner."

"Yes."

"Thick fluid leaking from your penis."

"A little bit, why?"

"Well, Mr. Johnson, your preliminary test results reveal that you've contracted a sexually transmitted disease called chlamydia." Silky was speechless so she continued, "Are you allergic to any medications?"

"No."

"Good," she said.

Dr. Lowe had written down all his answers on a questionnaire attached to her clipboard. Setting it down, she got up from her stool and put latex gloves on her hands. Lifting up his gown, she examined his penis.

"There are two ways to treat this. One would be orally, the other by injection," she said while inserting a Q-tip swab into his peehole.

"Ouch!" he screamed.

She pulled out the swab and placed it in a ziplock bag. Taking off her gloves, she opened the trash receptacle with her foot and tossed in the gloves. Washing her hands at the sink, she resumed writing on her paper, then filled out a label and stuck it on the bag.

"Mr. Johnson, it's very important that you use protection while being promiscuous. If you're having sex with more than one person, you have to use a condom. Now, you need to inform all your partners to get tested and you, young man, should practice safe sex."

"OK" was all he could muster.

"Which treatment would you like?"

"Run it by me again," he said.

"Treatment consists of taking antibiotics — penicillin, to be specific. To do it orally, you will have to take pills for seven to ten days. If I give you a shot the pain will go away, but you'd still have to take pills. Either way, you cannot have intercourse for at least a week."

"I'll take the shot," he said.

"OK, lay on your stomach," she ordered, putting on a fresh pair of gloves.

Silky rolled over on his belly then glanced sideways at the doctor. She stood squirting a drop of liquid from the largest needle he'd ever seen. Shivering at the thought of that needle piercing his ass, he gripped the sidebars on the table, closed his eyes, and waited for his medicine. Dr. Lowe wiped a section of his butt with a sterilized gauze pad, then injected the cold fluid into his body.

Dropping the needle into a red hazardous-waste container, she stuck a large square bandage on his behind, handed him a bag full of assorted condoms along with pamphlets on sexually transmitted diseases, and told him, "Practice safe sex next time. And no liquor until all the pills are gone. Good-bye, Mr. Johnson."

Silky slowly put his clothes back on, with his brain

trying to figure out how and who gave him the disease. Scooping up the bag of rubbers and pamphlets left by the doctor, he exited the clinic with his head down. Melody sat in the Mongoose reading the newspaper. Upon seeing his body language, she knew the results.

"You were right, baby," he said solemnly.

"Who gave it to you?" she asked sincerely.

"This bitch I met named Bridgette."

"So what? You're fucking her and me?"

"It was just one time," he sighed.

"Silky, that's all it takes. I tried to tell you the other night, don't be adding more hoes to your stable, but you fell asleep. If I'm to be your woman, you have to fire those bitches."

"I don't want the bitch — matter of fact, I'm of the mind to kick her ass."

"Just don't fuck her no more. Since you're special I'll give you one mistake, cool?"

"Cool," he said, relieved that she was still in his corner.

Silky took the city streets back to Melody's crib, driving at a snail's pace. By the time they arrived, he had given her the complete rundown on Bridgette, swearing he would never hook up with her again. Melody was angry at first by the fact he'd been with a "Snow Bunny," but she wrote if off thinking that the girl wanted to live out her fantasies.

He drove wondering if Bridgette was contaminated too, and did she infect her husband. And what about his own tongue, Silky suddenly thought. After all, he had used that on her vagina, licking her like there was no tomorrow.

They walked up Melody's stairwell holding hands. Silky was beginning to feel soreness in his behind from the medicine. Neither one noticed the black Cougar parked down the block, which had been shadowing them all day.

21
UNCOVERED
EVIDENCE

Tasha returned from Renee's funeral mentally drained. She'd spent most of the day grieving with the Butler family. Everyone knew who she was and about her relationship with Renee, but not all approved. Renee's family was full of relatives suffering from severe cases of homophobia.

Many ignored her presence outright, while others merely whispered evil words behind her back. The fact that she'd lost her companion didn't seem to matter — she wasn't really welcome there. When the clock struck four, she got up, said goodbye to Renee's parents, and left. As she drove away tears streamed down her face.

"How could people be so cruel?" she thought.

With her mind in a fog and feelings hurt, Tasha drove home, plopping down on her sofa before the door softly shut. Ten minutes later she was sound asleep.

Roger Foster reclined in the driver's seat of his sport

utility vehicle. To anyone walking by, it appeared he was taking a nap. Truth be told, he was doing what he did best, spying. Foster loved his job but hated this particular assignment because it separated him from his partner, Kyle McDavid.

McDavid had been assigned to Silky, while Foster trailed Tasha. Roger Foster was what officers aptly named the "new breed" cop. Young, black, intelligent, and from the streets, he used creative style while doing police work. The dude would take risks.

A healthy five-eleven, Foster sported a full-grown beard, cornrow braids covered by a black golf cap, mirror sunglasses, and black jeans, along with a loose fitting T-shirt. The black and white tennis shoes he wore were expensive, and he had one gold ring on each hand. Foster was a slickster blessed with the gift of gab. Growing up in the Sunnydale projects of San Francisco, he'd seen it all.

After about three hours, Tasha walked out of her apartment and got in her ride. She lived in a quiet working-class area of the city called Adams Point, which was sandwiched between MacArthur and Mountain Boulevards.

Tasha had shed her black funeral attire for a more comfortable green nylon sweatsuit and sneakers. She merged with traffic on 580, exiting at High Street.

Making a left on Congress, she pulled into the driveway of her dead uncle's empty house. Foster cruised past slowly, then an idea struck. If he was wrong, he could possibly lose her, but he just had to take the risk.

Driving around the corner to Fairfax and parking, he grabbed his miniature binoculars and clipboard, stuck a pencil on top of his earlobe, and put on a phony utility company shirt plus white hardhat. His role would be that of a meter reader.

Choosing a spot between two homes that provided an unobscured view of the rear of Tasha's uncle's crib, he looked at the gas meter, scribbled scratch on the paper attached to his clipboard, then peered through his binoculars. He focused on a window with the curtains pulled back, and the sight his eyes rested on brought a smile to his face.

Tasha was in the kitchen scrubbing away. She was cleaning a chair, mopping the floor, wiping walls, and washing dishes. Foster returned to his vehicle to call Johnson on his cell phone.

"Johnson here."

"Nate, I'm not certain but I think I may be onto something," he said as drove back around the corner and parked.

"Lay it on me, Roger."

"Well, the girl is in the house scrubbing her ass off in the kitchen."

"Oh really."

"Normally I wouldn't think nothing of it because people do wash dishes and mop floors."

"What changed your mind?" Johnson wanted to know.

"She seems to be wiping the paint off a chair, but didn't touch the others."

"OK Roger, you continue tailing Ms. Savoy and we'll secure a search warrant," Johnson barked. "What's the address?"

Foster gave him the address then heard the line go dead

before he even had time to say goodbye. Taking off his utility outfit, he drove back around the corner and sat down the block watching the home.

Johnson and Hernandez drove up an hour later, along with a three-squad-car escort. Tasha was on her way out when she saw Five-O roll up crazily with tires screeching to a halt.

"What's the meaning of this?" she angrily inquired.

"Ms. Tasha Savoy?" Johnson spoke calmly.

"You know that's my name," she sneered.

"I have a warrant giving me permission to search the premises." He showed it to her.

"Search for what?" She was indignant.

"I don't know!" He stared into her flaming eyes. "Maybe you'd like to tell me and save us all the trouble of looking."

"Be my guest, but don't tear up my uncle's home 'cause I know, and you know, you ain't gone find shit. What you need to do is find Renee's killer, that's what you need to do."

"That's right!" He snapped his finger. "I didn't tell you . . . we know who killed Ms. Butler."

"You do?" she was surprised.

"Yes, ma'am. The culprit's name is Skye Barnes. What we don't know is who killed him, not yet anyway."

"And you think I do."

"Do you?"

"Look man, do your search then get out."

"Alright boys," Johnson spoke to the waiting staff, "let's roll."

Tasha stepped aside, allowing the uniformed officers access, then smiled at the detectives and the small crowd of onlookers. Lighting up a cigarette, she inhaled the smoke then blew it in Johnson's direction. The officers scattered throughout the home and began ransacking it. Johnson and Hernandez headed for the kitchen along with Jimmy Chang, the number-one evidence technician.

Chang began spraying Luminol on the chairs, floor, table, and dishes. Closing all curtains and doors, the room was dark. From his bag Jimmy pulled a black light, which was nothing more than an illuminated scan detector similar to those fluorescent wands used to scan a body for weapons at public events and airports.

Luminol is a clear aerosol spray that police use to uncover hidden or washed-over blood. It can uncover blood specks that are unseen by the naked eye, even if they have remained dormant for thirty years. As Jimmy slowly scanned the room, blood drops were visible everywhere.

Retrieving a ziplock baggie from his evidence case, Chang scraped off portions of the chair, tile, and took the knife, which stood out like a sore thumb amongst the rest of the dishes on the drain board. Meticulous in his method, he flicked on the lights and proceeded to label every piece of evidence.

"What you got, Jimmy?" asked Johnson.

"Definitely blood, boss. Whose? I don't know until test results come back."

"I think I do." Johnson said, sure of himself. "OK boys, that's a wrap."

Everyone walked outside where Tasha was holding court with the huge crowd that had converged in front of the house.

"Now see, that's what I'm sayin, y'all ain't found shit," she boasted.

"Ms. Savoy?" Johnson spoke with authority. "You're under arrest for suspicion of murder."

"Man, I ain't killed nobody."

"You have the right to remain silent. . . ."

Johnson recited her Miranda Rights while Hernandez did a pat search, placed handcuffs on her wrists, then eased Tasha into the back seat of their service vehicle. The crowd diminished as onlookers peered through the window at Tasha, shook their heads in disbelief, and went home. She hollered her innocence to every passerby, then sat silent for the lonely ride to Five-O headquarters.

Kyle McDavid received a call from Foster telling him the assignment was over because Tasha was in custody. McDavid drove away from Melody's place smiling because he was tired and hungry.

"Roger, you're alright, dude!" McDavid shouted out loud.

Stopping to get a cheeseburger, Foster bought one plus fries and a shake for his partner, then drove to the station.

22
MELODY'S
IN CHARGE

Melody sat on the sofa next to Silky as he spent three hours professing his love. At first she was skeptical, but the more he rapped, the more she believed that he meant what he said.

"All I need is you, baby — you gotta trust me. This mistake will never happen again. You believe me, don't you?"

"Yes," she said truthfully.

"Now give me a hug."

He clasped her hand and pulled her up from the sofa then held her very tight. She melted into his arms like butter and began kissing his cheekbone. He wanted to kiss her on the mouth but remembering his lips were probably contaminated, chose otherwise.

"I need to go to the crib," he said.

"When are you coming back?" she asked.

"Probably tomorrow."

"Well, I'll go with you then. Let me get my things."

In one minute flat Melody had packed an overnight bag, blew out all of her scented candles, and stood ready to leave.

Silky took her hand and limped noticeably to the door. The penicillin shot was doing a number on his ass. Hobbling down the stairwell, he handed her the keys and told her to drive.

Melody started up the Mongoose then followed Silky's directions onto 580 to the 238 interchange. Connecting at 880, she exited on Marina East, made a left at Doolittle, and rolled to the Jamaican Arms.

"So this is where you live?" she said, impressed.

"Yeah baby, this is my spot. You're the only woman who's been here, so that should tell you something," he answered while limping through the courtyard.

"It does." She displayed all thirty-two while returning his keys.

Opening the door to his unit, he flicked on the lights. He thought he saw movement but it was too late. Silky's face slammed against the wall, courtesy of a powerful right cross.

"What the fuck...."

His words were stopped in mid sentence as blows rained on him from all angles. He covered up his face with his hands but the fists continued to pummel him. Melody's hand began furiously searching her bag.

"So you like white women, huh punk?" shouted Dino, armed cocked to strike again.

"Back up, motherfucker."

Melody closed the door as Dino and his two homeys stared down the barrel of her snub-nosed 38 Special.

"Sit ya ass on the couch foe I put a cap in you tricks," she snarled through clenched teeth.

"We don't want no trouble, lady," said Dino.

"You got trouble the minute you decided to jump my man."

"He isn't your man 'cause he been screwing my woman!" Dino whined.

Silky, who was now on his feet glaring at the perpetrators, fired a straight right to Dino's jaw, dropping him in a heap.

"Sit muthafucka, don't I'll kill you dead!" Melody wasn't playing.

Dino and his two henchmen sat on the sofa as Melody took over. Silky checked the back sliding door and saw that they had broken the glass to gain entry. He was happy she had insisted on coming with him because if she hadn't, who knows how bad he would have been beaten.

"Now, I know about him with your bitch, but she wanted his dick more than he wanted her stanky-ass pussy. That tells me you can't fuck worf a damn."

"Look lady...."

"Look mah ass! Baby, take this gun and if they move, blow 'em to hell. We gone get to the bottom of this shit." She handed Silky the revolver.

Silky trained the weapon on Dino, then casually pointed it at his pals. As each man stared death in the eye, they cringed. Melody lifted the phone off the receiver then handed it to Dino.

"Dial your house, asshole," she demanded.

Dino dialed his number and sat helplessly as Melody jerked the receiver from him, pushed the speakerphone button, and spoke softly to Silky.

"Honey, make her think this is a booty call. I don't care what you have to say, just get the bitch in here."

Silky didn't know what Melody had in store for any of them, but he damn sure wasn't going to cross her now. If it wasn't for her tagging along, he knew his ass would have been grass. Bridgette answered on the third ring.

"Hello?" Her voice was distant.

"Hey girl, how are you?" he asked, looking at Melody's angry face.

"I'm OK."

"Check this out, where's your husband?"

"He went fishing with his friends, but I can't see you anymore."

"You can't? Why not?"

"I think he knows something!"

"I don't care what he knows, you told me that I was your man." He glanced at Melody.

"I love you Silky, but I just can't see you anymore."

"OK, just let me talk to you for a minute because I know your mouth is saying one thing, but your body says another." He eyed Melody again.

"Alright, meet me in our secret spot. I can't stay long, though," she said.

"No!" He raised his voice. "You come to my place."

"But...."

"No if, ands, or buts about it. Just come, RIGHT NOW!" he yelled.

"I'm on my way," she said before hanging up.

Melody turned off the speakerphone, glared menacingly at Dino and his boys, then motioned for them to follow her into the kitchen.

"We'll see just what an angel your wife is." Her comment was directed at Dino.

She whispered in Silky's ear then led the three hoodlums into the kitchen, where she made them lie on the floor. Bridgette walked through the partially opened door and hugged Silky tight.

"I told him that I didn't want him anymore, then he did this."

She released her stronghold when Silky noticed she'd been beaten. Her lip was swollen, eye black, and she had lumps everywhere. She failed to notice that his face was swollen too. Silky unbuttoned her trench coat, revealing her naked body. Gobbling up her tits with his mouth, he pulled down his pants then told her, "Suck it."

Bridgette got on her knees and proceeded to play with his dick like a woman in love. Melody motioned with the gun for Dino and his boys to get up. Leading them into the living room, she forced them to watch as Bridgette's tongue licked up and down the underside of Silky's pole. Dino saw the size of his meat and cried out, "Stop it!"

Melody struck him upside the head with the butt of the revolver, watching with satisfaction as blood poured down his face. Bridgette recognized the voice, lifted her head away from Silky's dick, and turned around. The sight her eyes rested upon would remain with her for the rest of her days on Earth.

Dino stared at her with a pathetic look on his face.

Glancing at Silky's dick, he began crying. He imagined her accepting that large black piece of meat, which was two times fatter than his and at least ten inches long. Comparing it to his short six-inch pole, he dropped his head in shame. The fact that she was naked, playing with it, and had never so much as licked his ruined his psyche on the spot. He would spend the rest of his life feeling inferior to women. Dino was fucked up.

"Get up, bitch," Melody demanded, "and put yo goddamn coat on."

Bridgette stood up, buttoning her coat while staring at the gun pointed directly at her face. She looked at her husband with a pleading "I'm sorry" expression. Dino's homeboys felt stupid, realizing that they helped him because they thought Silky was wrong, but now knew that Bridgette wanted the nigger. Adding insult to injury, Melody made Bridgette sit next to Dino.

"Now first I think introductions are in order. My name is Melody and Silky is my man. He was just on loan to yo funky white ass, bitch." She waved the gun for emphasis. "I just wanted to prove to yo sorry-ass man that you fell in love with that phat-ass black dick, 'cause we both know you ain't never had nothin like that before, right?" She demanded an answer.

"Y-y-y-yesss," Bridgette stammered.

"OK, what you say yo name was?"

"Bridgette," she whispered.

"Girlfriend, you're in love with my man, right?"

"No, I mean, I guess."

"You in love wit his ass, right?" Melody hollered.

"Yes, I love him!" Bridgette blurted out.

"And, let me get it right. You love him 'cause he fucks the shit out of you?"

"Yes." Bridgette thought about Silky's penis. She was now calm.

"You enjoy that BIG black dick sliding in and out of your tight asshole, right?"

"Dino could never make me feel that way," Bridgette said as she stared at her nails.

"Oh my god!" Dino screamed.

"Shet up, punk!" Melody whacked him upside the head with her gun again. "Hold my shit, Silky."

Melody wiggled out of her skirt, ripping off her blouse at the same time. Standing stark naked in front of them, she resumed her rap.

"You." She pointed at Dino's friend. "What's your name?"

"Karl," he said.

"With a C or a K?"

"K-a-r-l, ma'am."

"Do I look worthy of fucking?"

"Yes ma'am."

"You want some black pussy?"

"I don't know, ma'am." He glanced at Silky, who was confused by it all.

"Take off your clothes, Karl with a K."

Karl was Dino's lifelong buddy, and the two were closer than brothers. He stood six feet two, was handsome and chiseled. He stripped down and stood in front of them embarrassed.

"Bridgette, take your coat off and lay on the floor," Melody demanded. "Karl with a K, you fuck her."

"Right here?" Karl asked, shocked by the request.

"Yeah, right here, fool!" Melody shouted.

Karl lay on top of Bridgette and began kissing her slowly. Her kisses forced him to think of how much he always secretly wanted her, causing his dick to swell up with blood. Dino sat looking with eyes wider than a dope-fiend's on crack. Karl penetrated and plowed away with the freedom of knowing he was "forced" to do it.

Bridgette's eyes rolled into the back of her head and she began humping like an untamed horse. Dino sat crying like a bitch, watching his woman enjoy his best friend's meat better than she'd ever enjoyed his. Silky was amused by it all, knowing Bridgette would never forget him. Melody pointed to Dino's other friend Jamie and told him, "You ain't seen shit, right?"

"Lady, I don't know a thing." His hand stroked his cock, eyes greedily watching.

"OK, I hate to break up a good thang, but y'all ghit ya ass outta here."

Melody slipped back into her skirt and hugged her man. Karl and Bridgette put their clothes back on while Dino and Jamie rose to leave. Dino had the look of a defeated man because Bridgette's body language suggested that he was out anyway and Karl was in.

"Listen up, y'all," Melody quietly stated, "if you fuck wit me or my man again, I'll kill ya, understand?" They nodded in agreement, knowing she meant it.

Marching out single file, they headed back to Dino and

Bridgette's place, happy to be alive. One year later Bridgette and Karl were married, and three months after that, they had the first of four children. They named the girl Melody.

I STAND ALONE

Tasha sat handcuffed to the chair staring at four walls. She had to urinate and knew her bladder couldn't hold it too much longer. Still steaming from the booking process, which required her to strip down and be inspected by female officers, she wondered what evidence they had gathered to charge her with suspicion of murder.

She had scrubbed everything clean with bleach, but the Chinaman with the upside-down-pyramid-shaped head frightened her soul. He looked like he knew his business. Rising up from her chair, she attempted to move the table but found it dead bolted to the floor. Lifting her leg up, she kicked the door furiously.

The door opened slowly with Johnson, Hernandez, and uniformed officers peering in, ready for action.

"I have to use the bathroom," she said.

"But you don't have to damage property to tell us," Hernandez stated.

"If you'd take off these damn handcuffs I wouldn't have to do that shit," she spewed.

Johnson summoned Maria Jimenez, who was writing her report on Shakey's death, and asked her to escort Tasha to the ladies' room. Uncuffing Tasha's wrist from the chair, he led her down the hall. Maria walked side by side with her while Hernandez trailed behind. Maria punched in the code numbers on the door, then entered the restroom. Hernandez placed a foot in the doorway, keeping it partially open so he and his partner could hear but not see what was going on.

Tasha flushed the toilet, washed her hands, then was led back to her interrogation room by the three detectives. Once again, they created a triangle, leaving no avenue for escape. Not a word was spoken during the entire trek. Nate thanked Maria, who resumed her report-writing, then he and his partner followed Tasha into the room.

Hernandez softly closed the door behind them and pulled out his micro-tape, pressing the record button as he sat it on the table.

"OK Tasha, why'd you kill him?" Johnson asked bluntly.

"Kill who?" Tasha played dumb.

"Skye Barnes."

"Who?"

"Look young lady, you killed him and we know it."

"Man, I'ont know what you talkin about." She shrugged.

There was a knock at the door so Hernandez hit the

stop button on his tape player. It was Jimmy Chang, standing there with a stoic facial expression. Tasha felt a lump
rise in her throat.

"HIM," she said to herself, "what the hell he wont?"

Jimmy threw his head to the side and walked away as
Johnson trailed him out the door. Hernandez re-cuffed
Tasha to the chair and joined them in the office, closing
the door.

"What's up, Jimmy?" asked Johnson.

"The blood type found in the kitchen is the same as
Barnes, but I won't know for certain until the DNA test
tomorrow."

"What about the dirty fingernails on Barnes?" Maria
chimed in from her seat.

"Jones' blood," Jimmy answered.

"So Skye killed Shakey, then Tasha killed him?" Johnson quizzed.

"Looks that way, boss," said Jimmy.

"Thanks Jimmy, you're a real pro, man," Johnson said
while shaking his hand.

Maria smiled broadly because her first homicide case
was solved easily. She was going to enjoy this job, or so
she thought. Manny shook hands with Jimmy, then Maria
followed suit. Chang walked out the door as if he were
Five-O's guardian angel. Johnson and Hernandez re-entered
Tasha's room with attitude. Hernandez pressed record
then took over the proceedings.

"Look Ms. Savoy, you might as well come clean 'cause
we got you nailed."

"You ain't got shit!" Tasha shouted. "I don't care what

that dude told you, I want my lawyer." They knew she referred to Jimmy.

"Here," Manny offered her his cell phone, "call your lawyer."

"I ain't callin nobody!" Her eyes were like a raging inferno.

"Just as I thought, you'll be represented by a public defender."

"Fuck you."

"Now now, Ms. Savoy," Hernandez enjoyed this, "calm down, OK? Here's the way we see it. Skye kills Renee but the bullet was meant for Duane — you call him Silky. Somehow, Skye finds Shakey Jones before you find Skye, and kills him too. Next, you kill SKYE!" His voice rose three octaves. "His blood was all over your uncle's house, and since your uncle is dead and you're the caretaker...."

"Man, it wadn't no blood in that house."

"Yes, there was," Hernandez whispered before Johnson took over.

"Tasha?" Nate played good cop.

"What?" she returned.

"Are you familiar with Luminol?"

"What?"

"Luminol, are you familiar with that?" he repeated.

"No, I'm not," she said.

"Luminol is the substance we sprayed in the kitchen. What it does is uncover blood specks hidden from the naked eye. Your uncle's kitchen revealed traces and gobs of blood on the chair, floor, and this knife." Johnson showed her the weapon. "Now our preliminary findings are that the blood belongs to Skye Barnes."

"OK, I did it!" Tasha cracked.

"Who helped you?" snapped Hernandez.

"Nobody."

"Oh, you carried him out to the car by yourself?"

Tasha flexed a muscle on her arm, which bulged into a rock-solid lump. It looked more powerful than most dudes'. The detectives knew she was capable of carrying Skye on her shoulders.

"Yeah, I carried his ass."

"Where did you leave the body?" Johnson quietly asked.

"On Fiftieth, the train tracks."

"Then what did you do?"

"Then I went for Toothless, but I guess you beat me to the punch."

"So you knew at the club that those two were responsible for Renee's death?"

"Yes, I knew." She was now solemn.

"Why didn't you tell us that night?" Johnson showed concern.

"That niggah killed the one person on Earth I truly loved, so it had to be an eye for an eye."

"Why kill the old man?" Hernandez asked, puzzled.

"I didn't kill that old dude," she answered.

"Who did?"

"The hell if I know!" Tasha started crying. "All I killed was Skye 'cause he killed Renee. I ain't answering no more goddamn questions!" She began bawling like a baby.

At her trial Tasha played on the jury's sympathy, claiming that she killed Skye out of love for Renee. She was convicted and sentenced to serve twelve years in the women's prison at Chowchilla. The charge of premeditated murder was reduced to murder in the second degree. She never uttered a word about Silky and Junebug's involvement.

On her very first day of incarceration, she strolled through the yard receiving pats on the back from all of her Oaktown homegirls. A young, high-yellow woman named Louise approached her with tears in her eyes.

"Thank you," she said.

"For what?" Tasha asked while standing ready to rumble.

"Killing that asshole. I loved Renee too."

Tasha embraced Louise, holding her tighter and longer than necessary. Using the back of her index finger to wipe away teardrops falling from the small woman's eyes, she led her to a quiet corner of the yard.

"Don't cry baby, everythang's all right now."

Tasha lifted Louise's chin up, stared into her eyes, then tongue-kissed her lovingly.

FILED AWAY

Johnson and Hernandez never did find old man Reese's killer because the murderer left no clue. That homicide would remain opened and unsolved forever. Beverly Reese sued the city for a one-million-dollar wrongful death claim, to which the city agreed before the case ever went to trial. She lived the rest of her life in luxury, not to mention adding another notch to Ralph Givens' belt loop.

Givens held a press conference in front of City Hall, ridiculing the police force for sloppy work. He didn't care that all of the week's past murders were solved except one, only that he'd successfully represented yet another client. His legendary status was growing rapidly in the black community. Word on the street had it that if you had a case, Givens was the man.

"Who do you think killed the old man?" Johnson asked Hernandez.

"I think it was the girl, Nate."

"The girl? Tell me, partner, how did you come to that conclusion?"

"See, amigo, Tasha drove away from the club that night but for some inexplicable reason rode back by — that's when she saw us outside talking to Reese. Lying in wait, she watched us leave, went in, then stabbed him."

"Do you have any evidence to back up that ridiculous claim?" Johnson eyed his partner.

"No I don't, but I think that's how it went down and until I find any shred of proof to suggest otherwise, that's what I'll always believe." Hernandez was convinced of his theory.

Johnson laughed so hard that his stomach began to hurt. Hernandez was happy to see his partner smiling again, which caused him to join in on the laughter. The waitress brought their dinners and smiled at the two detectives having fun, then sauntered off. Hernandez ate his enchilada while Johnson devoured his super burrito. As usual, they ate in silence.

HOMECOMING

Sweetpea stood in the corner sipping on a glass of wine while scanning the room. The party was jumping, with liquor flowing freely. Everyone was dressed to the nines, proudly displaying their finest attire, along with the most expensive pieces of jewelry they possessed. No one knew him and he would keep it that way — after all, his reputation depended on it.

He wore a black tuxedo, dark shades, fake mustache and sideburns, along with an expensive brim pulled down low on his forehead. Sweetpea, elegantly blending in, was on assignment. This particular job called for him to observe only. Anyone fidgety or looking out of place would be taken care of with the quickness.

The parking lot of the social hall was overflowing with luxury cars, and attendants took extreme caution not to put so much as a fingerprint on them. No one said it, but they knew if they erred at this function, it could well be their last.

Food was plentiful, the dance floor packed, atmosphere festive, and cocaine floated around on serving treys as if it were legal. A white stretch limo cruised slowly in front of the building, parking in the space reserved for it. The room got quiet and dark, with people placing their index fingers in front of their mouths and blowing for silence.

The front door opened with the lights flicking on simultaneously. The band began playing Kool & the Gang's "Celebration," and the party resumed in earnest. Cameras clicked photos nonstop, broad grins covered all faces, and everyone converged on the guest of honor. Sweetpea slipped out a side door, got in his Benz, and headed home — his services would not be needed tonight.

Big Ed stood in the doorway impressed by his homecoming party. Displaying all thirty-two teeth, he laughed loudly. It was good to be home.

Questions or comments, email Renay:
LADAYPUBLISHING@CS.COM

Thanks for your support!!

ABOUT THE AUTHOR

Renay Jackson is a former rapper and street lit author with five novels to his credit, all of which will be published by Frog, Ltd. over a two-year period. Jackson received the Chester Himes Black Mystery Writer Award in 2002. A single father to three daughters and a niece, he lives in Oakland, California, where he has been a custodian for the Oakland Police Department for more than twenty-five years.

Photo by Frank Alliger